The Spring Rider

The Spring Rider

JOHN LAWSON

A Harper Trophy Book
Harper & Row, Publishers

The Spring Rider
Copyright © 1968 by John Lawson

For information address Harper & Row Junior Books, 10 East 53rd Street, New York, N.Y. 10022.

LC Number 68-17079
ISBN 0-690-04785-1 (lib. bdg.)
ISBN 0-06-440349-1 (pbk.)

Published in hardcover by Thomas Y. Crowell, New York.
First Harper Trophy edition, 1990.

FOR CHARLOTTE

CONTENTS

CONTENTS

It is said that in the spring, in April, a rider comes up into the mountains from the east, from the Shenandoah Valley and beyond. He is often seen in the distance—a very long thin man in a high stovepipe hat, in black clothes, on a horse too small, and his feet dangle below the belly of the horse. In the distance he is familiar and you know you will recognize him when you come closer, but when you come around the corner he is not there.

CHAPTER I

JACOB

THE WAY to the log barn where the lambs were lay through the small meadow. Jacob walked hunched against the early morning cold with his hands in his pockets. He had tucked the bottle of milk inside his blue denim jacket. He could feel it warm there. He walked with head down. Sometimes he kicked the old hard piles of cow droppings. He stopped once to turn and watch the smoke drifting lazily from the chimney of the house, hanging still and gray above the glistening roof. No breeze came to take the smoke away and it hung there forsaken. This was a sign of changing weather. It had been a late spring, and maybe now it would come. "It doesn't have a choice," he had told his mother, who had been worried about the hay holding out. "Spring will never come," she had said and cried. Jacob was twelve and he knew spring would come.

The morning would come. There was no holding it back. The air was cool with dew and stars. And separately, there was the wood smoke. The sun had not yet risen above the mountains to the east, but already it was reaching its white light. The sky was dark blue. The stars to the west stuck to the blue ceiling of the world like dying diamonds, and the moon hung palely in between.

The way to the log barn lay across the field where the battle had been. When Jacob had been young he had thought the whole Civil War had been fought in his meadow—one long battle up and down the meadow, night and day, for years and years, in and out of dreams. But now he knew it had been just one battle, one day, and maybe not even a big battle. The North had been here in the bottom where the empty hay pens stood. The South had been on the top of the ridge where the new sun hit and turned the dew to light. The North had attacked, been beaten back, and then routed by the Southern counterattack. That was when Colonel Turner Ashby of Stonewall Jackson's cavalry had jumped his horse over a hay pen in Jacob's meadow. This was where the killing had been done, where Jacob stood. There was a pine tree there dead, killed they said by the blood from the battle of a hundred years ago. Its bare branches scratched the cool air.

There were dark patches on this field, and this was where they said the blood had sunk into the ground and made it rich. Sometimes Jacob had seen that these dark green patches were in the shape of men—

curled up, stretched out, and in funny shapes. Sometimes on misty mornings when the clouds were low —not like this morning—Jacob had thought to see men rise from the ground and stand in the mist.

This morning the lambs had found the sun and lay stretched in it against the side of the barn. The three ewes searched for new grass. Each of them had triplets. They were good ewes and would have enough milk for three lambs when the grass came, but only on old hay they wouldn't have enough milk.

Jacob scooped up one of the lambs and sat down with his back against the barn. He had the milk in a big old brown whiskey bottle with the regular black rubber nipple you can get for lambs. The sun was warm now. The lamb poked at the bottle to make the milk come faster. The lamb braced his legs to get a better pull. Jacob closed his eyes. He opened them when the lamb gave too big a pull and almost knocked the bottle out of his hands.

Jacob sat up. This was one of the big lambs. Usually with triplets there were two fine lambs and one small one. The small one was the one who needed the extra milk. A ewe has only two teats, and sometimes after the two biggest lambs have sucked, she won't stand for the third. He should have given the milk first to the small ones. There was one real weebly. Jacob was angry just to see it standing around with its head down swaying. This morning the lamb was lying against the barn. It was never going to amount to much. The head even seemed too big for the neck to lift.

Jacob picked the lamb up suddenly and shoved the nipple roughly into the mouth. He tilted the bottle up too sharply, so the milk came out too fast and almost choked the lamb. The milk dribbled out of the side of the lamb's mouth and stood in heavy white drops on the tightly curled wool. Jacob shook his head. It was his fault. A lamb is a lamb. He was glad that his mother or Gray was not here to have seen. His sister was most fond always of the weak lambs. They were always the ones she wanted to see. Jacob didn't mind the sick lambs. What upset him were the weebly ones who wanted to die and usually did. Jacob sighed and took the lamb in his lap and gently worked the nipple in again and let the lamb suck slowly. It didn't take much. Jacob withdrew the nipple.

At that moment Jacob first heard it—a rustling that seemed to come from the barn loft. Was it a bird nesting in the hay? Jacob listened. He could hear the run on the other side of the barn. He could hear the old sycamore creak. He could hear the sheep cropping.

The lamb stirred in his lap. The throat beat in his hand beneath the short tight wool. He tilted the head to see the eyes. This lamb might live. The ones that wanted to die said so plainly with their eyes.

Jacob gave the nipple again slowly and let the lamb want it, made it arch the neck and reach. Jacob leaned back against the barn to feel the sun. The lamb drank in long sleepy swallows. The spring was coming, like he said. There was a way he could turn his head in the sun and he could feel the spring on one cheek and the winter on the other. He set the lamb up so that he could take off his jacket. The lamb stood for a moment with all four legs out straight, and then he shook himself. It was a way strong lambs had when they stood up. Jacob looked for one of the other weak lambs.

That was when he heard the noise again. There was someone there in the barn loft. Jacob was not frightened, but he slipped around the side of the barn so that he was away from the hole cut in the logs for an entrance to the haymow. Jacob leaned against the barn. He made a face at a lamb that came poking around the corner. This was a good old log barn. It was good for hay because there was lots of room between the logs for the air to reach the hay. Jacob waited, but nothing came.

It was easy to climb up the side of the barn. He went quietly, making sure each time that he had his grip on the big log above. He was careful when he reached near the top that he didn't go above the level of the hay for then he could be easily seen. He got his final hold and raised his head very slowly to peer through a crack into the barn.

The top of the barn above the logs creaked with the slightest breeze. Old wasps' nests were plastered like gray dry paper in the corners. The tin roof snapped and popped on the brown strips. The mice ran mincing on the rafters and furred into holes. The warmth of last summer and the moistness of last spring were caught in dry blossoms and sweet dust. The sun slanted in. From the far corner of the mow there was a moan. It was over there where the sun slanted in and the peaks of hay tossed like pale waves.

Then Jacob saw the head and shoulders come half out of the hay and then one bare arm stretched out like a swimmer on his way from sleep to life. The white thin shoulders of an oldish boy and the big browned hands of a farm boy. The neck and face were tanned. Orchard grass and timothy were mixed in his hair. He shook his head like the lamb and stretched. He sat up and, brushing the hay from his hair, looked around carefully. For a moment Jacob thought he might have been seen and ducked his head down and just hung to the side of the barn very still.

When he looked up again, he could see that the boy had put on a cap—a soldier's cap, a peaked blue soldier's cap. He followed this with a soldier's jacket. And soldier's pants. Blue soldier's pants he wrestled into on the hay, first on one leg and then the other, and then falling down entirely in the hay. Jacob almost laughed.

But he didn't, because they had come. He had always known they would, but not like this, not a soldier alone asleep in this old barn. With blood and noise he had thought they would come and many together. And not a young soldier either. The battle had always been fought for Jacob by big men with black beards and old men with gray beards. He had never seen any boys like this rise in the mist from their bed in the meadow. But this soldier had to be one of them.

He watched the soldier take a gun and then a bugle and then a pack from the hay and pull all this toward the mow entrance. Jacob saw him look out cautiously and then jump down. There was nothing for Jacob to do but to stay hanging to the side of the barn. The soldier passed beneath him. He seemed in full uniform now. He had his pack on. He carried his gun slung over his shoulder. He carried his bugle in one hand. He whistled.

Jacob knew the soldier was one of them.

CHAPTER II

HANNIBAL

JACOB WAITED until the soldier had gone well around the corner of the barn before he dropped down to the ground. Carefully he looked around the corner. The soldier seemed to be heading toward the small hill beyond the run. The soldier stopped, knelt down, and scooped up the water to his face. Then he stepped back and with a great leap cleared the run, sailing with outstretched arms and legs. Jacob's view was partly blocked now by the sycamore, and he ran around to the other side of the barn to watch. But he couldn't see here either, and finally he climbed up into the haymow.

He could see the soldier very clearly now as he went up the hill. The soldier's hair was long, and it curled over the back of his collar. His canteen bounced against his hip. Jacob crunched down farther in the hay. Up the hill the soldier went, leaning into it and stopping once or twice as if he were tired.

And then, on top, he stopped to turn and look all around. He didn't seem to find what he was looking for. Finally he took the bugle from his shoulder. He banged it against his thigh, shaking out the hay. He spit a couple of times. He blew on his hands.

He brought the bugle to his lips and pointed it at the sky. "Come to me, come to me," it cried. It echoed up and down the valley—a long sweet cry—and died. "Come to me, come to me," it cried. And it called Jacob. It called him with shivers up his back. And he crunched down farther in the hay to keep the shivers there and to keep from running out to meet the bugler.

Soldiers would come from far away to answer such a call. Long blue lines would come with flags ahead and officers on horse. Columns of men winding like snakes between the hills. Bugles would answer and bands. The blue coats of the Union. And if they came, wouldn't Stonewall Jackson's nut-brown champion marchers of the Confederacy come through the woods like locusts? And wouldn't Turner Ashby of the black beard come on his white horse?

But no soldiers came now. The bugler stood alone on the hill. Jacob crawled around the mow and looked in all directions. The sheep still moved bowed to the grass against the hills. The cows still stood at the salt box licking their lips with slow rough tongues and switching their tails at the first flies. The calves closed their eyes and curled into warm balls. The road still twisted with glistening pools down the hollow.

The bugler on the hill spit on his hands again. He blew it softly—"Come to me, come to me." And then again fiercer. It was lost like a new cloud in a big windy sky. A sudden gust came and shook the sycamore by the run like a child. The soldier waited a moment and then came back down the hill toward the barn. Jacob was afraid of being discovered. He was afraid of hiding. He was afraid the soldier would get away before he had a chance to talk to him. Jacob climbed down the ladder. And then he sauntered around the barn with his hands in his pockets. He watched the soldier leap the brook again. Jacob stood his ground by the barn waiting. It was his barn anyway.

The soldier looked older as he came closer. He had baggy knees. He wore his cap down over his eyes.

"Morning," Jacob said. He said it sooner than he meant to.

The soldier kept coming closer. He seemed to look right through Jacob with pale blue eyes. His uniform was clean but faded and worn. The face was not as young as he was. "You see any one like me around?"

"You're the first," Jacob said. He knew what the

soldier meant. "But the others—they'll come, I know."

"How do you know?"

"I heard you call them. I was in the barn, and you were on the hill, and you called them."

The soldier took his gun and pack and laid them against the barn. "You know bugle calls?"

"You really did call them."

"I can blow better." The soldier went over to the run and knelt down, splashing water in his face.

The gun was there alone and it was only a second for Jacob to grab it. He had it firm in his hands when the soldier turned, shaking the water out of his hair.

"Hands up," said Jacob.

The soldier put his hands up slowly like he talked. "I hope you know how to use that piece."

"I guess I do," Jacob said. "It's just an old gun, isn't it?"

They stood like that for a moment.

"I could lock you up in the barn," said Jacob.

"You could."

"You're a Yankee, aren't you?"

"Yup."

"I thought you were. When I first saw you, I said to myself, 'He's a Yankee soldier,' even though I never saw one before."

The soldier nodded.

"My great-great-grandfather fought with General Jackson, and I guess he killed a whole lot of Yankees." The gun had begun to droop, and Jacob lifted it sharply.

"I expect," said the soldier.

"You're not so bad—for a Yankee, I guess."

"I got a real itch," said the soldier.

"You might scratch one-handed." Jacob watched as the soldier unbuttoned his jacket and scratched. "That's what you get for hiding in the hay in our barn."

The soldier buttoned himself up again and put his arm up again.

"Maybe you better just give me your word," said Jacob.

"To do what?"

"To do nothing. You just give me your word."

"If I don't?"

"Is there going to be a battle? I bet that's what's going to happen. There's going to be a big battle, and you can't tell me."

"Could be."

"So I'll just take your word," said Jacob. "Because if there's going to be a big battle you wouldn't want to miss it."

"I'm not going to fight in any battle if I don't have that."

Jacob held out the gun to the soldier. "I bet it's going to be a big fight."

The soldier took the gun and put it back with the pack.

Jacob picked up the soldier's cap from where it lay by the barn.

"You are a picker upper," said the soldier.

"Second Maine." Jacob put the cap on. It came down pretty far.

"Like this." The soldier straightened it so that the cap came down over Jacob's eyes and the visor rested on his nose. And then he fixed his feet and hands. The soldier suddenly sprang to attention. "REPORT!"

"Huh?"

"You're meant to identify yourself."

"Jacob Downs, Ashby's cavalry, uh, uh, Jackson's Army, the Army of the Valley of Virginia and . . . the Confederate States of America."

The soldier took the cap back. "Like this," he said. "REE-PORT!" he said and snapped to attention. "Sergeant Hannibal Cutler, Third Squad, Fifth Platoon, Company B, Forty-fourth Battalion, Thirty-third Regiment, Second Maine Division, Eighteenth Brigade, Fourth Corps, Army of the Potomac of the United States of America."

CHAPTER III

THE MAP

"THAT IS SOMETHING!" said Jacob. "Do you say that very often?"

Hannibal was going through his pack. "No." He shook his head. "Most of the time they just call your name, and you say, 'Here.' " He pulled a big biscuit out of the pack, knocked it against the barn. "Shakes out the worms," he said. With both hands he broke the biscuit in two and handed half to Jacob. "Hard tack," he said.

Jacob tried to take a bite and grunted.

Hannibal spread out a map on the ground. It was an old, many-times-folded map with the lines of the folds crisscrossing it into squares.

"Don't taste much," said Jacob, nibbling at the edges of the biscuit.

"Not meant to." said Hannibal, smoothing the map out all the way. "Where are we?"

Jacob had not seen many maps. There was one in the Bible where the Mediterranean was edged with small waves and had big waves in the middle. He did see a big X at one place, and looking closer, he saw it was near the Forks of the Rivers. "Why, that's the Forks of the Rivers it says, and that's near the Devil's Backbone."

Jacob got down very close with almost his chin on the map. It was amazing how it was all there. He put his finger on the road out of Blue Grass valley through the gap where the Devil's Backbone arched in granite down the mountain then into the valley of the Jackson River. Jacob traced and twisted his finger along the road where the sycamores marched in single file like white ghosts along the river bank. He stopped once at the old plank bridge.

"Go on," said Hannibal impatiently.

Jacob crossed the bridge very fast. He slowed down a little bit on the edge of town where the map was frayed, but from there on it was easy. "It doesn't show our road," he said. "But here's the run! And here"—with his finger on it—"is where we are!"

The soldier took an old stub of a pencil and licked it and made a big smudgy X at just that place. Jacob noticed that there were lots of old X's that had been erased here and there.

"I guess you've been in this country before."

"I guess I have," said Hannibal, sitting back, nodding to himself.

A lamb wandered between them as if he were going to look at the map and find out where he was.

Jacob picked him up and half threw him to the side. He didn't want any lamb to make a mess of Hannibal's map.

"He wants some milk," said Hannibal. The lamb had found the bottle on the grass where Jacob had left it.

"They always want some milk," said Jacob. He didn't want to talk about lambs now.

Hannibal picked up the bottle, and he picked up the lamb. He settled himself against the barn with the lamb in his lap. "There now, old lamb," he said. "That's it," he said very slowly. "That's it."

"I don't guess there will ever be any more real wars, do you think?"

"I expect," said Hannibal. He had his hand around the neck and chest of the lamb and had the head tilted up just right. The lamb closed his eyes and took long gulps. "This bottle is not so warm," he said.

"Are you going to a battle? Is that where you're going?"

"We never kept sheep. People did. But we never kept any." The lamb had sucked enough. He licked his lips. Hannibal kept him in his lap for a moment and then he set him up and let him go. Hannibal leaned back against the barn for a minute with his eyes closed against the sun. "But I never remember any lambs like that. I never knew they came so small."

" 'Cause these are all triplets, that's why."

Hannibal opened his eyes and didn't move his head from where it rested against the barn. "Is that the road to the Big Sinks?"

He was looking toward an old log road that ran into the woods beyond the mountain. In the openness of still early spring you could see it twisting up the mountain, and you could see it high up where it stood out like a white shelf cut into the mountain.

"It's not much of a road," said Jacob, "but it's not a bad one either."

Hannibal yawned. "If I stay here I'll be like that lamb." The lamb had lain down. Its big stomach beat up and down, up and down. Its tongue stuck out pink. Hannibal got up and stretched. "I've got to be going," he said.

"Maybe I might just go a ways with you."

"You might." Hannibal was gathering his things together.

"I could carry something—like the gun or the bugle. I could carry the bugle."

"You can carry the gun. Nobody but me carries the bugle. Not anybody."

"That's because you call them."

"That's because I call them."

"And do you send them away?"

"I could," said Hannibal. "I could."

Hannibal took long slow strides. Jacob had a hard time keeping up. "Look," he said, "there you can see where some of the battle was, the one they stopped the Yankees in and then drove them clear back up the Franklin Valley."

"I might just look at that place one day."

"I'd show it to you. Any time you want, I'll show it to you. I'd do it right now."

"Can't now. Haven't got time now. And you have to go back."

Jacob handed over the gun.

"You might just not tell your people that you saw me," said Hannibal. "They might not understand."

"I wasn't counting on it."

"Well," said Hannibal.

"See you," said Jacob.

"See you," said Hannibal.

They each turned and walked a little way from each other.

"Hey," said Jacob, "I could come with you. I mean all the way. I could come to the battle."

Hannibal shook his head. "No," he said. "No, you can't. You can't come."

"Maybe I could just watch?"

"Can't nobody watch."

"You were in the war, weren't you? You were one of them, weren't you?"

Hannibal nodded.

"And Ashby will be there? He'll be at the battle?"

"I expect," said Hannibal.

Hannibal stood looking across the farm where the

shadow of a small cloud was sliding over the pasture like a big hand.

"Good-by, good-by," Jacob said.

Hannibal waved.

And now suddenly Jacob knew how late he was. He ran down the road. His mother or his sister Gray would be looking for him.

And Gray was standing by the barn as he came out of the woods. Her skirt billowed. Her hair, not white like his but blond, was gold in the sun. She had her hands stuffed deep in her pockets the way she did when she was angry.

"Where have you been?" she said, almost before Jacob was close enough to hear her.

Jacob put his hands in his pockets. "In the woods."

"You didn't even finish the milk."

Jacob didn't say anything.

"Why do you do this, Jacob? Why do you always do this?"

They walked back through the meadow with the long stilted morning shadows slanted beside them. Gray put her arm around Jacob's shoulders. He did not go from it, but he squared his shoulders so that there was no softness.

"Jacob, Jacob," she said, "what do you want?"

And that was a silly thing to say: "Jacob, Jacob, what do you want?"

"Mother was so worried when you didn't come

back. And then you didn't even give the lambs their milk."

In the full sun the blood spots were dark green on the meadow. The new grass was matted there. The dew stood on it in a thousand hard drops. "Do you think," said Jacob, "that Turner Ashby ever rode right here, right through our meadow?"

"That's what they say."

"If he did again, and he could—you said yourself that everything was possible—if he did and wanted men to join him, I would."

"Well, he's not going to."

"I didn't say he was."

"All Mother thinks of is you, Jacob. You're the only man she has."

Jacob looked to the mountain where the log road scarred its long white twisting way. High up where it shelved he saw a lone blue figure moving slowly. The sun hit something metal, and for one instant there was a diamond on the mountain.

CHAPTER IV

GRAY

GRAY WAS WAITING. Sometimes in the morning after milking and before the day began she would do this —come down to the edge of the road at the bottom of the hill, climb the fence, and wait. She was young. She was pretty. She had gold-brown hair. Her lap was full of crocus blossoms. She had brown eyes with no doubt in them. It had only been the spring before when she was sixteen that she had started waiting. Someone would come down the road to her, for her—and carry her off? Probably. It would have to be someone passing through, and he would want to go—with her.

She did not move or even look in his direction when she saw the Spring Rider come down the hill. She had seen him from the distance many times. She waited to see if he would disappear. She kept very still on the fence with her eyes down and only her fingers moving among the crocus blossoms in her lap.

She heard the hoofs of the horse come close. "Good morning, Miss," the Spring Rider said. He tipped his tall black beaver hat low to her, full down. "Might I tie up here for a moment?"

He was even taller when he stuck his hat on top of the fence post and bent over. He leaned on the top rail of the fence and looked up the hill to where the old Southern breastworks still ridged across in front of the trees.

"This is where the battle was," Gray said. "The North was here along the road." Gray had heard it many times. "And the South was up there on the top of the hill."

"And where were you?"

"Me!" she laughed. "Why that was long ago! Before me."

"But where would you have been?"

"I would have been way up in the mountain where the dogwood is and had my hands over my ears. That's where I would have been. But my brother—my brother would have been up there with Ashby."

The sheep were coming down the mountain now on their slanted path terraced out of the slope by ten thousand hoofs on a thousand mornings. They came in a white line like pilgrims. The young lambs cluttered the path, stepped off, clambered back, stepped off, came down the hills in high leaps over shadows and rocks. As they leapt they tucked their forefeet in as if they never expected to come down.

The Spring Rider looked across the mountains where the service trees were white and the dogwood blossoms fanned out. The new sun caught the red rust in the dogwood blossoms.

"It's where they crucified Him," Gray said.

"How's that?"

"The dogwood blossoms. Didn't you know that? A dogwood blossom is like a cross, and at the end of each petal there's like a nail hole with rust around it. It's where they crucified Him."

"I never heard that."

"I'm surprised. Everybody here says so."

"I'll remember. It's been that I loved the dogwood in the mountains."

"You look at them real close. You'll see."

"And you believe it?"

"It's always been so for us," Gray said. "It's not like you who didn't know." She looked down the road where it stretched brown, still damp with dew, waiting. There was no one coming.

"Who are you waiting for?"

"Oh, just someone." She looked down the road in the other direction.

"You think he'll come?"

She looked him right in the eye. "He'll come."

"You'll recognize him when he comes?"

"Of course. He'll come, and I'll know."

The Spring Rider smiled, but the sadness was still

there. Part of the sadness was that he was so ugly with a mouth too wide and a nose too big and eyes buried too deep above the cheekbones.

He untied the reins of his horse from the fence. "You'll need two kisses," he said.

She sat up straight. "Why two kisses?"

"You don't know? It's a saying I thought everyone knew."

"Not around here."

He climbed on his horse. He put on his hat. "It's what you always tell people in love. 'You'll need two kisses.' " He looked down at her to see if she knew what it meant. "Some people," he said, "think it means that you need one kiss to meet and one kiss to say good-by—but I don't think it means that. No, I think it means just that one kiss is not enough."

"I don't think it means that, either," Gray said, frowning seriously.

"It may not," said the Spring Rider amiably. "It may not. I don't know."

Gray jumped down from the fence. She brushed the last of the blossoms from her skirt. "They call you the Spring Rider."

"Why do they say I come?"

"I asked my mother once, and she said she knew once or her daddy knew but it was forgotten."

"It doesn't matter. In the beginning I came out that spring to find the bodies that lay alone and forgotten away from the road. And now I hear the shooting and the shuffling of the armies in the dark and the crying of the wounded for water after the battle is over. They come here in the spring from Gettysburg and Chancellorsville and Chickamauga and Shiloh. And they fight among themselves again. These are the ones for whom it mattered. That's why I come—to stop them."

"Why don't they stop? Why do they go on fighting and fighting?"

"Why does the dogwood have rusty holes?"

Gray shook her head. "But to keep fighting! I think it's silly."

"I don't know what it is," the Spring Rider said. "But it isn't that."

"Why do you care?" Gray said. "Why do you give yourself misery for it? If they want to, they will. People always do what they want to do."

The Spring Rider almost smiled. "If that's true, then I must be doing what I want to do."

Gray didn't say anything. Her eye was caught by the first butterfly of spring. It was yellow and black, and she had been forgetting how hard a butterfly must beat its wings.

"A black and yellow dress," Gray said. "If you eat the wing of a butterfly, you get a dress like that. If it's a black and yellow butterfly you get a black and yellow dress. If it's green and gold you get a green and gold one."

"And have you done that?"

"I have," said Gray.

"I think I must have eaten nothing but black butterflies," the Spring Rider said. "Black ones. All black."

"I don't do it anymore," Gray said. "Eating butterflies is for little girls."

"Yes," he said. "I guess that's so. We have other things to eat." The Spring Rider turned his horse on to the road and then came back to where she was standing. "When he comes," he said, "don't let him get away. It would be a shame to waste all that waiting."

She flung her arms about herself and hugged herself tight. "He won't get away."

Gray watched him out of sight and then went up the hill to the top where she was going to look for ginseng. The ginseng was a root that made Chinamen fall in love. That was why people here dug it and sold it, so that it could get to China. You dug it in the fall, but in the spring it was easy to spot. The Chinamen ate it, people said. Gray had wanted to taste it once, but she hadn't for fear she would fall in love with a Chinaman. Jacob had tasted it. "Bitter," he said. And then he had put a finger to each eye and pulled them into slits. "Am I getting yeller, Gray?" he said and stuck out his tongue at her.

"You're bitter, Jacob," she had said. "But maybe even you will fall in love someday."

CHAPTER V

THE PINE TREE

"WILL YOU BE QUIET," whispered Jacob fiercely, "or you're not going to see my old fish."

"I never did care about your old fish," said Gray. "I only came because you wanted to show it to me so much. And now it isn't even there."

They were lying on their stomachs on a limestone ledge above the river at a place where a deep pool lay. Jacob had discovered all by accident one day that from here he could see right down to the bottom of the pool where the big trout lay. At a certain hour he could see the round sun at the bottom, a perfect gold circle.

"He's just under the bank. He'll be out," said Jacob, squinting down. From here the bottom of the pool was clear to every rounded rock next to rounded rock, even to the sands that lay flat and still beneath the running stream.

Gray looked down the river, where it curved in dappled sun beneath the dark pines. Here there was no bottom of nestling brown pebbles or smooth sand, only a rolling surface of quicksilver or dark shadows layered out of sight.

Jacob turned his head to glance at Gray as she stared down the river. "Now who did you see this morning? I know you did. Cat's got your tongue all day."

Gray dropped a pebble into the pool. Beneath its erupting circles it dropped through the clear water in a long, wavering fall. "And if I did, I wouldn't tell you, Jacob Downs."

"And if I told you," said Jacob slyly, "and I told you who you saw, then I guess you might tell me what he said."

Gray picked up another pebble and held it suspended over the pool.

"You saw—" said Jacob slowly. "Don't go dropping things like that," he interrupted himself.

"All right," said Gray, throwing away the pebble. "What did I see?"

"You saw a soldier, a Yankee soldier, name of Hannibal."

"That's who *you* saw, isn't it?"

Jacob looked at her, crestfallen. "You didn't see him."

"And you saw him this morning, didn't you," said Gray, "when you were so long with the lambs?"

"Who'd *you* see?"

"I'm not telling."

"That's not fair!" said Jacob, sitting up. "That's not fair! I told you. And now you've got to tell me. That was the bargain."

"Bargain? What bargain? Let's go. I just came to see your fish."

Jacob turned to look down again at the pool. "If you'd stop throwing rocks at him, you might see him."

"One little old pebble."

"There—see him?" said Jacob. A big brown trout glided out from under the bank and took up his position against the current.

"I see him. He is nice. I don't know why you don't catch him now."

"In May. When the May flies hatch. That's when I'm going to catch him. If someone doesn't find him first."

"Don't look at me," said Gray. "I'm not going to tell anyone."

"I know who you saw," said Jacob suddenly. "I know who you saw. You saw the Spring Rider. That's who you saw! We used to see him from the pine tree. We used to—remember? When we were young." Jacob could smell the pine tree. He could feel the stickiness of the pitch.

Gray reached out to drop a pebble and accidentally hit Jacob in the nose with her elbow. "Poor nose," she said. She hugged Jacob, and Jacob hugged her back. She looked at him in surprise. "Why'd you do that?"

"You hugged me first. Why'd you do that?"

"I like to," said Gray. "But I forget to. You're such a man grown."

"I forget, too," said Jacob. "But I remember. When we were young."

Gray dropped the pebble. The trout darted beneath the bank. The pebble fell wavering to the bottom where the sand danced in memory of the trout's tail.

"Remember," Jacob said, "in the pine tree we saw the Spring Rider once. It was about this time of year, and we were up in the pine tree and we saw him. We saw him coming down the road on his small horse with his big hat. And then he disappeared. And we asked about him. And someone said, 'Oh, that was the Spring Rider.' "

"I remember," said Gray. "I remember we used to go up in the pine tree."

"We'll go now. Just like we used to," said Jacob.

"The tree is dead," said Gray.

"Come on," Jacob said. He grabbed her hand and pulled her. "Maybe we'll see the Spring Rider! Maybe we'll see the Yankee!"

Gray let herself be pulled along. Jacob ran. So Gray had to run, too. The ewes on the hill above the river looked up in surprise. The lambs ran. The calves danced away. Out of breath Gray and Jacob hugged the tree. The rough bark scratched Gray's cheek.

"Come on," said Jacob. He had already pulled himself up onto one branch.

"I can't."

"Come on." Jacob reached down and pulled her up. They went on up like that. The pine tree had died but the branches were still there, sticking out sharply from the trunk.

"It wants to be climbed," shouted Jacob.

"It missed us," called Gray.

The dead tree still smelled pine. The trunk was pocked with woodpecker holes.

"I guess the old woodpeckers really like this old tree," said Jacob. He looked up and he looked down and he looked far away. "How many?" he said to Gray. "How many worms in this old tree?"

Gray looked down. "I don't want to ever go up any more."

"You old scairdy cat. It isn't even where we used to go."

"Yes it is," she said. "It's higher."

"I can show you," said Jacob.

"No. Don't, please," she said.

"Look," said Jacob. "Look how clear you can see the blood spots in the meadow."

"I've told you before that is not what they are," said Gray.

"That's what they are."

"What did the soldier say?" asked Gray softly.

"We just talked. He had a map. I showed him where he was."

"I'm sure."

"I did!"

"The Spring Rider is a sad man," she said.

"That soldier, too," said Jacob.

"I want to go down."

"Watch!" said Jacob, and he pretended to fall. He caught himself so that he was hanging down from the bough by his hands.

"Stop it!" screamed Gray, frightened.

"Watch!" said Jacob laughing, and he worked his way out along the branch.

And then he swung. He swung in long slow arcs. He was stretched long. His winter-white chest and arms glistened. His eyes were closed. Sometimes he shook his head to shake the hair out of his eyes. Gray was no longer afraid for him. She would not have been surprised to see him fly. And he swung back and forth like that in the falling light.

CHAPTER VI

JACKSON

It was the night wind that brought the sound up the valley. The sound of harness jingling and weapons, the sound of a thousand hushed noises and shuffling feet, and then a clear word breaking out from the rest, picked up alone by the wind and delivered to the foot of Jacob's bed.

Jacob tiptoed across the cold moon floor to the window and looked down the valley where the black mountains ranked solid against the clear cold sky. At night the blue sky is lifted from on top of the world where it has sat all day like a bowl turned down. The world is not flat at night. At night the mountains are not the top of the world but the edge of the world. At night the world spins through the stars and the lights dot out one beyond the other. The full moon hangs like a cold round stone in the sky.

Jacob dressed. He stole down the creaking stairs and hushed the noises with his toes. He paused in the warm kitchen where the coals glowed in the fireplace. The room was quiet as it never was, as it waited for the morning. A mouse scurried in the corner. A fly buzzed against the window to reach the moon. This was another room.

Jacob slipped out the door, shutting it firmly. The sound was on the main road. He could tell that. Up the hill he went in the moonlight. The moon was so bright it turned his shadow into company. The locusts by the road made shadows, too, that swayed like long flowers against the pasture. Two haystacks, left over from the winter, stood solid on the meadow, stood like gigantic acorns on the field of moonlight.

From here on the hill Jacob could see the log barn. The log barn was old silver. The roof was shingled with silver bits. The haymow was a dark mouth. The wheels of the hayrake at the corner of the barn were ten feet tall. It had come from the moon a chariot that night. The thirty-foot-high horses were in the shadows. And the breeze that came along the mountain now had been brought clear and cool from the moon and smelled like that.

Jacob crept the last way up the hill. He lay flat on the top and peered down to where the main road twisted dusty beside the jeweled river.

A thousand-legged dusty caterpillar was moving down the road. An army was moving down the road. The men lurched in single file along each side of the road. Their backs were hunched with packs. They carried blankets in horseshoe rolls across their shoulders. They marched asleep with slouch hats. Down the middle of the road came the canvas-covered wagons. Here and there a new cover shone white in the moonlight. The artillery came with wheels taller than the men who walked beside them asleep. A drummer boy rode on the end of one large piece. He bobbed up and down, a seesaw rider. Along the middle of the road came an officer now, shouldering between the wagons and the walking men. There was no end and no beginning.

Jacob could see the line stretching dusty as far as the road went. It was a sable army. Even the dark night and the bright moonlight could not change the nutmeg brown of this army asleep, coughing its way through its own dust down the valley. Every once in a while a single figure would break ranks to run down to the river to fill his canteen and then run back up the bank and along the file of men until he found his own place among the sleepwalkers.

Jacob did not know how long he lay on the hill and watched the army. But he did stay until the General came along. It must have been the General, because even the wagons stopped to let him by easily and several officers came along behind him.

The General pulled up on a little knoll by the side of the road. The horse stood still, black, growing bigger in the moonlight as Jacob watched. The General and the officers wore gray. They wore dark black boots above the knee. The General took off his gray slouch hat and rested it in his lap. His beard was dark. Only his forehead shone in the moon. The gray uniforms were almost white. The horses shook their heads and the metal at their mouths lighted.

The General reached out one hand to let it rest, stilling, on his horse's neck. The men shuffled along the road, heads down, not even aware that he was there. The horses of the officers behind him skittered impatiently. The officers took off and put on their gloves.

Jacob ran down the hill toward the road. He tried to stay in the shadows, but he was in too much of a hurry to really take care. He followed the line of an old fence encrusted now in briers to the road. And then he was almost on top of the little group of officers. He could smell the horses.

Suddenly he felt a hand on his shoulder, and he was dragged out of the briers and across the fence.

"And what have we here?" asked the General.

"We found him in the bushes, sir. He was spying on us."

"I wasn't spying," said Jacob, shaking himself loose. "You wouldn't have caught me if I'd been spying. I was just watching. I just wanted to see who was who."

"And did you decide—who was who?" asked the General, looking down at Jacob.

"Yessir, you're General Jackson, but . . ."

"But what?"

"I was just wondering where Colonel Ashby was."

"You know the colonel?"

"No sir, but Colonel Ashby would be on a white horse, I think, and would not be in the shadows. He would be next to you."

The General had been watching his army down the road. He seemed to be impatient and tired now of the small talk. "The colonel is not with us. He is scouting ahead. We have only lately arrived in these parts."

"Where are you going?"

The General turned from the road to look at Jacob. Without even turning to his aide he said, "Put this man under arrest. He's a spy."

It happened so quickly that Jacob was taken completely by surprise. The General had his hat on and was pulling on his gloves.

"May I say one word to the General—in private?"

"And why in private?" asked the General.

"Because," said Jacob, "I remember now hearing how you kept all your plans to yourself and never even told anyone where you were going. So if I just started talking about where you were going, you might get so mad you'd shoot me instead of just arresting me."

"I hope for your sake it's worth my time."

Jacob walked up very close to the General's horse. With his hand he could feel the horse breathing. The General leaned down from the saddle.

"You're going to the Big Sinks," said Jacob, "and there's an easier way than this."

The General straightened very sharply in the saddle. "Come with me," he said and sharply turned his horse through the small group who had been standing aside while Jacob spoke to the General.

The General led the way to his headquarters wagon standing at the side of the road. They climbed in. The General carefully buttoned up the flaps at the back of the wagon.

There was a built-in table along the center with benches on each side. The General lit a candle, and the place was filled with shadows in the corners and in the canvas top. The candle was gold. Jackson's beard was red gold. He took off his gloves and slammed them down on the table. He took a large map from inside his jacket and spread it out on the table, pressing it flat with his big hands, as if he could solve all his problems by pressing the lines out of the map.

His eyes were blue. "If you're a spy, sir, you're a bold one—but no help that will be to you. And what makes you think I'm going to the Big Sinks?"

"I saw a Yankee this morning, and that's where he was going. That's where he said the battle was to be."

Jackson leaned back and stared at the ceiling where the shadows danced. "To be sure," he said. Then abruptly he leaned over the map again. He had the biggest hands Jacob had ever seen. "And how would you go the Big Sinks, sir?"

Their two heads almost met over the map. Jacob could not figure out where they were on the map. It appeared to be all upside down. He took it by the sides to turn it. Jackson was leaning on it. "Excuse me," he said, lifting his elbows and not putting them down again until Jacob had turned the map the way he wanted it.

"Ah," Jacob said, pointing to the Springs.

"I would say we were here," said Jackson, pointing with a stubby finger to a place where the road made a long curve.

"No," said Jacob, who knew where he was now. "You're a long way from there. That's where the rough place in the river is. You're back here. This is where you are." Jacob put his finger down firmly.

"It's not such a difference," said Jackson defensively. He moved the candle to the center of the table. "And where is your way to the Big Sinks?"

"Here," said Jacob, "is where it is. It doesn't show on your map. It's an old logging road."

"There is the artillery," said Jackson.

"If it's no bigger than what went down the road a while ago, it won't stick."

Jackson leaned over the map again. He measured

the distance with his finger. "It's about two miles from here."

"Yessir," said Jacob, "you must have gone right past it."

Jackson was silent for a moment. He stroked his beard. He smoothed out the map again. He looked at Jacob and his blue eyes never moved. Jacob could see the candle in them. "If you had come to me with this two hours ago, there would have been time to look at your road and then make a decision." Jackson stroked his beard again. "But now it's a matter of turning the whole army around and heading them up a mountain road that may not exist following a young man who is not even one of us."

It seemed unfair to Jacob that the blame should all be put on himself for not having come two hours earlier when the General should be grateful that he had come at all. But Jacob didn't say anything and just looked at the map.

The General leaned back and put both hands flat on the table. "Do you know your Scripture? Ananias. Who was Ananias?"

Jacob had felt very sure of himself as long as they had been talking about roads, but the Scripture was something else. It wasn't that he didn't know it pretty well. It was just that it all went out of his head when someone slammed his hands on the table and said, "Ananias. Who was Ananias?"

"Uh," said Jacob.

"Do I have to tell you what happened to Ananias?"

That rang a bell. "Struck dead he was," said Jacob. "He and his old woman. Just like that."

"Why?"

"For lying. He lied about money."

"Money. Maps. What difference does it make? Lying. Ananias was struck dead for lying. Find it." The General slid an old Bible toward Jacob. "Find it and read it to me. I want to hear you read it."

Jacob opened the Bible. He remembered it was in a chapter with a strange title. He came upon a dog-wood blossom pressed dry. He looked up. The General was sitting back on his bench with his back against a post. His eyes were closed. His chin was up. His arms were folded against his chest. His beard was red gold, and the light danced at the end of his hairs. His gold buttons glimmered.

Jacob kept going. There it was! Acts! Here it was at the top of the page: Ananias and Sapphira. Jacob wondered if the General was asleep. He had heard that the General could go to sleep like that. Just asleep all of a sudden. Jacob wasn't going to awake him if he was asleep. Jacob kept his eyes on him and his finger on the place so he could read right away if the General woke up. That was what happened. One of Jackson's eyes opened for a moment. One blue eye shone out. The lid went down.

Jacob read. Very fast he read: " 'But a certain man named Ananias, with Sapphira his wife, sold a possession, and kept back part of the price, his wife also being privy to it, and brought a certain part, and laid it at the apostles' feet. But Peter said, Ananias, why hath Satan filled thine heart to lie to the Holy Ghost, and to keep back part of the price of the land? Whiles it remained, was it not thine own? And after it was sold, was it not in thine own power?' "

He was reading very fast now, and Jackson held up his left hand as if to halt him. And then Jackson spoke very slowly: " 'And after it was sold, was it not in thine own power? Why hast thou conceived this thing in thine heart? Thou has not lied unto men, but unto God. And Ananias hearing these words fell down, and gave up the ghost: and great fear came on all them that heard these things. And the young men arose, wound him up, and carried him out, and buried him.' "

The General stopped and was silent. His eyes were still closed. Jacob idly turned the pages. In Corinthians he found a red maple leaf aflame with fall. The General reached for the Bible and took it and held it for a moment in his big hands as if he would squeeze something out of it. Suddenly his hand moved out and in a flash of light Jacob saw his thumb and forefinger close on the candle flame and pinch it out. A flash of last light and fingers. Darkness. Silence.

Jacob could feel the grained ridges of the table top with his fingers.

Then he heard. "Preserve us, O God, for in Thee do we put our trust and it is Thee we would follow. Thou wilt light the candle I have snuffed out. May the Lord my God enlighten my darkness and lead me to the Big Sinks."

Again there was silence. And then suddenly the flap at the back of the wagon opened with scraping boots, and General Jackson jumped down into the moonlight and set his spurs spinning silver.

CHAPTER VII

ASHBY

IT WAS ALMOST at the top of the mountain that Jacob heard the horse for the first time. He was at the head of the army. He looked back. General Jackson rode asleep behind him, lurching half sideways in the saddle with one shoulder lower than the other, with his gray slouch hat pulled low so that he had no face but a beard and a hat. There was mist here on the mountain and Jackson's breath steamed.

Behind Jackson the army stretched down the road, long in sound but out of sight except here and there in the half moonlight where the road took a turn out of the woods onto a shelf. In the shadows and the woods there was a glint of steel now and then, or in the open places there might be a white face caught suddenly looking up met by the moon. But there was always the sound of the army, of harness and hoof, and coughing, and shuffling feet, and the heavy wheels of the artillery, and now and then the sudden swearing of a man who stumbled. And finally all of it became one sound, the steady breathing of a headless animal crawling up the mountain in its sleep.

When they had started, Jacob had felt the leader. He was leading the way. But now this army had gone to sleep, even Jackson, and if Jacob were to stop, it would not, but would simply go on as it was going and run over Jacob. But it would follow where he went. He was the eyes of the animal.

One horse with quickened step in the shadows did not belong. It was moving faster than the army. It was moving faster and faster. Then Jacob, looking down, saw the gray rider come across the shelf of moonlight on his white horse, disappear into the shadows, lost except for the sparks from the hoofs. Jackson still slept.

The white horse was coming closer now. Jacob could hear it clearly now. Jacob did not turn to watch it now or slow to wait for it. He went on his own cool way.

"Make way! Ashby's coming through! Make way!" It was a low, strong voice and carried in the silence. "Jackson! Where is General Jackson?"

"I am right here, Colonel Ashby. And I and everyone else can hear you perfectly." The General did not look up. If he had not spoken, you would have said he was still asleep.

Ashby reined up beside the General and brought

his horse alongside, so they rode knee to knee behind Jacob. "You can't take the Army over the mountain on this road, sir."

"And why not, Mr. Ashby?" said Jackson looking up and looking around. "And why not? We would seem to be almost at the top of the mountain now. Isn't that right, Mr. Downs?"

"Yessir," said Jacob, half turning so that he could get a look at Ashby. He saw a tall, thin man in a loosely fitting light gray uniform with very bright gold buttons and high black boots and black gauntlets and a black slouch hat and a very black beard. His face was dark.

This was Colonel Turner Ashby—the eyes and ears of Jackson's army. This was the courtly Ashby who rode a white horse along the horizons. This was the man called "the Arab."

"And who the devil is Mr. Downs?" asked Ashby.

Jackson did not even turn his head. And when Jacob saw that he wasn't going to answer, he turned ahead.

"I was hasty," said Ashby, "but who is Mr. Downs?"

"Mr. Downs came to me with some very interesting information. And"—the General coughed to himself—"he suggested that there was a far easier way to get where we wished to go rather than the out-of-the-way course advised by some."

"This road is not on the maps, sir."

"And since when has Colonel Ashby been limited to roads that are found only on maps?"

"But to trust the army to a stranger, to a mere boy, in the night?"

"And if, Mr. Ashby, a stranger were to be sent to us to guide us and aid us and we shut our hearts against him because he was a stranger, do you think we would be deserving of His help again?"

Ashby pulled his gloves on tighter. "Let's hope the road goes down the mountain as well as up."

"Oh, it does," said Jacob, looking back. "This road really goes down on the other side."

"You're aware," said Jackson sharply, "that our artillery can find such a road very difficult—perhaps impossible. I didn't bring this army up here to lead it down again like a reverse-the-circle dance."

"Oh, no," said Jacob hastily. "It's not like that. It's just a good dropping road. It's not level, but it's not what I'd call really steep."

Jackson didn't say anything. They were at the top now. Jackson held up his hand. He didn't even turn around. And the army, the crawling animal, came to a grudging halt. Then the three of them rode off the road into the grove of locusts that grew there. It was a shallow place, and they were careful as they came to the rocky edge.

"Ah," said Ashby, drawing in his breath as if to taste with his lungs this new air from the other side of the mountain. He stood up in his stirrups as if he wanted to take it all in. They were at the very edge now. Ashby's horse was skittish and moved back nervously.

"Yes," said Jackson, "they are there before us. See the fires, Mr. Ashby."

The Big Sinks lay stretched below them checkered in moonlight and shadow, in rolling hills and hollows of darkness where the mist rested. And at the very farthest were the fires dotted like candles. Jackson was awake now. He held up his left hand, palm out, the way he did so often when he was excited. His horse skittered close to the edge. Without taking his eyes from the red glow, he reached out and stroked the horse's neck. "Yes," he said, "yes."

"A long way away," said Ashby.

"It seems so," said Jackson. "Very far away. And then it seems that I can see the shadows about the fires. And I think I can hear those people."

"I'll tell you how close they are soon," said Ashby.

"You will not go alone. Where are your men?"

"They're coming, sir."

"Coming, Mr. Ashby? What does that mean? I sent for you and your men."

"I thought perhaps, sir, that your message might have been in error and I came on ahead."

"And what good is Ashby to me alone? I want to know about those people." Jackson waved toward the Big Sinks where the campfires glowed like dawn.

Ashby's face turned to black shadow.

Jackson glanced at him. "You may take Mr. Downs with you. He knows the way. I want both of you back at daybreak."

Without a word Ashby wheeled his horse and was off down the road, making sparks. Jacob looked at Jackson. The General nodded in the direction of the road. "Tell Mr. Ashby—when you catch him—that I do not wish him to be headstrong."

"Yessir." Jacob wheeled his horse with an Ashby flourish and almost dropped the reins. The horse seemed to stumble. Jacob was glad it was dark. Down the road he went as fast as he could with only the sparks ahead to lead the way.

CHAPTER VIII

THE RIDE

IT WAS a ride down the mountain. Jacob's horse seemed inspired by the occasional glimpses ahead of Ashby. After a couple of curves where Jacob felt sure that they were going off the edge, he shut his eyes and put his head against the horse's neck. He could hear with one ear the horse's heart measuring and with the other the hoofbeats on the road. And almost with his nose he could touch the road. Each hoofstep was like an earthquake that shook the ground. With his hands on the shoulders he could feel the road coming up to meet his hands. As long as he could feel that, he kept his eyes shut.

Sometimes low branches brushed his shoulders. And sometimes he could tell when the road went through the pine-dark part of the forest where the air was cool. With his eyelids he could feel the cool darkness rushing. Here it was quieter with the hoof-beats lost in the pine needles. And then out again onto the shelves that curved open around the mountain in the moonlight. Here the rocks scattered and he never heard them hit. Here the moonlight lay like bright running finger tips on his eyelids.

With his cool cheek in the wind he could feel where the sky began. And then with his fingers he felt the shoulders stretching out into a long sloping gallop down a straight piece. It was where the road down the mountain ended, and Jacob opened his eyes.

He was in the middle of what seemed to be a very large open sinkhole. The road forked here. There was little moon, and even when Jacob got down to look closer for prints, he could tell nothing. It was strange to stand and walk. He was stretching when he saw it—a glow, a red glow at the base of an old chestnut that stood rotting on the horizon of the sinkhole. Jacob saw the glow breathe larger and then suddenly almost disappear.

And then he heard a tree frog mock him with a sad warble. "Yes, old frog," he said to himself. Two fingers to his lips, he warbled back to that sad tree frog. "Yes, old frog," he said as he wondered. He had seen, too, in that half instant of glow the face of a man. It didn't seem possible that Ashby would have had time to settle himself there with his cheroot.

But he had. He was sitting with his back against the tree, calmly pulling on his cheroot as if this was what he had come down the mountain for. One leg was cocked over one knee and his hat was perched on the foot.

He got up to greet Jacob. "Ashby, Turner Ashby at your service, sir. I apologize for my rudeness up there with the General, but it's been a long day and I just wasn't ready for the idea of turning the whole army around."

"Oh, that's all right," said Jacob.

"Have a seat," said Ashby as he settled himself down. "I was wondering where you were."

"I think I'll just stand. I haven't had a chance to get off that horse in quite a while."

"That's the way it always is at the beginning of a campaign. And later on it will be strange to be off the horse." Ashby blew a smoke ring at the moon and cocked his head to watch it.

"I figured you were in pretty much of a rush."

"I'm always in a rush," said Ashby, "but I always slow down when I get close. It's like a dance. The fast whirl is fine for getting acquainted, but it's the slow turn that does it. Are you a dancer, Mr. Downs?"

"No sir, I never have. But my sister, I guess, can dance most any man off his feet if he dares to take her up. I have heard that said by several people, and some you wouldn't think to hear say it."

Ashby sighed. The cheroot glowed. "Never much of a dancer myself. Just between us, I think I preferred horses." Ashby laughed to himself. "There isn't any time for that anyway. In fact it's very seldom that we run into people like yourself at all. Not that we're not happy to. It's just that we don't. We pretty much come and go and mind our own business along the way."

"I met one of them, too," said Jacob. "Came from Maine, a bugler," Jacob told him. He walked around Ashby and told him. Ashby lay with his back against the tree and listened.

"Did you now?" said Ashby. Puff. "Second Maine." Puff. "Know them well." Two rings. "No dash, but very good solid people who keep coming at you until there aren't any more of them left."

Jacob hunkered down beside Ashby. "You should have heard him call on that bugle. I bet he could call the spots off a hog. 'Come to me, come to me' —he called like that. I bet he could call the pennies off a . . ."

Puff.

Jacob didn't say anything.

"Off a dead man's eyes. The pennies off a dead man's eyes."

"It's a saying around here," said Jacob. "I hope it's no offense."

"No offense with me," said Ashby. "It's just as well to understand what company you keep."

"I knew," said Jacob. "I knew when I first saw him and when I first heard him. Our place, you know, is where they fought that big battle. And sometimes when we make garden we find bones. And I'll say to my sister, 'That's a Yankee bone.' And sometimes I think I hear the fighting in the night."

"Should be buried—all the bones should be buried."

"Oh, we bury them. My sister wouldn't have one in the garden—a bone, I mean. Not just Yankees. You can't tell the difference anyway."

"That's what's so bad. I heard my granddaddy talk of killing Indians once, and he said it wasn't any more than killing flies."

"Or Chinamen," said Jacob.

"That's just what I mean," said Ashby. "Just what I mean. But this war is the real thing. Those people are just like us. Could be your brother. Or your father."

"Could be a cousin."

"Could be any number of cousins. Could be a whole regiment of cousins."

Jacob shook his head. "But they'd shoot you, too, wouldn't they? They'd kill you just as dead?"

"Don't you doubt," said Ashby, as he stretched. "But, you know, after they'd done it they might cry about it. They might feel very bad about it. There wasn't anybody very happy about it after they did it."

Ashby buttoned all the buttons down to the very last one of his jacket and threw away his cheroot. "And do you know why that was? It was because they were like us and we were like them. Now you take Old Jack, he knows that. I said to him once—think it was near Port Republic—I said something about how brave the Federals were fighting. Old Jack called me on it. His eyes were blue like china cups. 'Mr. Ashby, I do not wish them to be brave.' That was just how he said it. 'Mr. Ashby, I do not wish them to be brave.' Now, do you know why he said that?"

"Sure. He wanted to win the battle. He wanted them to run away."

"Part of it," said Ashby. "Part of it. But the real part of it was that he didn't want to have to kill them. That was the real part of it. He was going to have to kill them if they acted like that—and he didn't want to."

"And he would, wouldn't he?" said Jacob.

"He surely would. You've never seen him when the fire's up. That's when we call him Blue Jack. His eyes turn blue like china. People who see him as you saw him tonight say, 'Why, Stonewall Jackson's a sleepy old fool who doesn't say a word or even hear what you're saying.' Wrong, all wrong! They haven't seen him when the fire's up. They've seen Old Jack. They haven't seen Blue Light."

"He sure doesn't like you to ask where he's going," said Jacob, shaking his head.

"Isn't that for true," said Ashby, swinging himself up into the saddle. "Are you ready?"

"Ready," said Jacob.

"I'll ride a little bit ahead. And if I raise my right hand like this—you see?—you stop where you are. If I raise my right arm up and down like this, you come on fast, and if I raise my left hand, you take off—you understand?—you just leave. You take yourself back to Old Jack and tell him that Colonel Ashby may be detained."

"I wouldn't do that," said Jacob. "I wouldn't leave you detained."

"You'll do what you're told if you ride with me."

Jacob nodded. Ashby rode on ahead—turned, smiled, and waved Jacob forward.

CHAPTER IX

THE BRIDGE

ASHBY LED the way into the Big Sinks. There was no road, but it was easy for Jacob to follow the white horse as it picked its way among the fallen trees and between the brush. Its breath steamed, and the white tail flicked at the moonlight on the great rump. Jacob had been in the Big Sinks before but never at night with a cold moon in the sky and the sinkholes full of shadows.

Jacob knew that in the day the land rolled easily as far as you could see, pocked with the sinkholes that gave it its name. There were brooks and even small rivers that sprang full born from a bank and ran twisting—and then disappeared as suddenly into caves. And Jacob had heard it said that one day the whole thing, the whole Big Sinks, might collapse into the big river that ran beneath. There was one big river that ran beneath the Big Sinks, and it ran underneath the mountains to the sea, and where it came out, the salty ocean was clear and cold for miles around. Where that was, Jacob didn't know except that it was true.

The night was cold now, and Jacob could feel the reins turning hard in his hands. They picked their way through spiked brier patches where dry trapped leaves rattled. They went through a locust grove where the moonlight left long drifting shadows on the ground and dark fingers across Ashby and his horse. It seemed to Jacob for a moment that Ashby had turned to a statue on his horse beneath the moving trees. Then Jacob went into the shadows and felt his horse lift his legs high and swish his tail.

"Stop!" He heard it whispered.

Jacob had not been watching ahead as he went through the shadows, and now suddenly he found himself almost on top of Ashby who had stopped abruptly on the crest of a hill. Ashby had not even turned. Then Ashby motioned Jacob forward beside him.

They were on a small ridge, and below them was a river white with the moon leading away from them. Mottled sycamores stood guard along the banks where the shadows were. And not far away from the hill on which Ashby and Jacob were was a bridge—a bridge of silver weathered wood blotting out the moon. The river slid black beneath it, but around the pilings it frothed white.

The bridge was empty but on the far side of the river was a small fire where soldiers stood with their gigantic shadows. And far away was the Union Army. Its campfires glowed in a great circle that filled the horizon. They were close enough now to see the individual fires and to see the smoke curling into the cold night.

"How deep is the river here?" asked Ashby.

"Pretty deep. And the banks are steep."

Ashby nodded. "They wouldn't be guarding the bridge if there were other ways to cross."

"It's going to be pretty hard to get across that bridge."

"Um," said Ashby. He didn't say any more but led the way back down the hill and out of sight of the bridge. Then they went along the side—always out of sight of the bridge but always nearer the bridge until they knew they were close because they could catch voices and hear the fire pop. Ashby was moving his horse very slowly now.

"I'm going across," said Ashby. He spoke quietly and gently. "You wait here. And if I'm not back by dawn you can take the word to Old Jack."

"I'm coming with you," said Jacob. He was prepared to say much more if he had to.

But he didn't. Ashby looked at him. "As you wish. Keep up with me. I don't like looking back."

"I'll be there," said Jacob.

"Um," said Ashby as he slowly pulled his gloves tighter. "All right. No time like the present, eh?"

And suddenly with a twist he turned his horse up

the hill, and in an instant he was over the hill and out of sight. Jacob didn't hesitate. He was more afraid of losing Ashby than he was of the soldiers on the other side of the bridge. "Ai-y-ee" he could hear Ashby with the rebel cry down the other side of the hill. And then Jacob was tilted down the hill behind Ashby, already on the thundering planks, and the fire was bright ahead.

There was a shot.

"Ashby! It's Ashby!" There were two shots and he heard one go by and bury into a post along the edge of the bridge. With a leap Ashby cleared the fire, and Jacob took his horse that way too because he wanted Ashby to know that he had followed him. And as he jumped the fire Jacob saw a shoe left to dry by the edge of the fire. It was steaming. That was what he saw.

And now they were riding away from the fire. Jacob could feel his back wide and long behind him and he tried to flatten it out. Three shots. Like quick birds. "Let Ashby go! Get the other one. Don't shoot Ashby." Two more shots. They were out of the light and into the darkness. For a moment Jacob thought he had lost Ashby, but then he saw the big white horse at the top of a hill ahead. Jacob felt his own horse climb into the hill, and there just over the crest was Ashby waiting for him.

Ashby held up his hand for quiet. "Listen," he said.

Jacob's heart was beating too full for him to hear anything.

"I didn't see any horses there, did you?"

"I don't think so." There had been no horses there—except Ashby's white pinned forever above the flame. And Jacob himself there. He could see that, too. He could see himself on his red brown arched above the flame.

"That's fine," said Ashby quietly. "If they had horses they would be after us by now. They'll have to walk to camp. And we'll be there long before them."

"Did you feel the fire when you jumped it?"

Ashby smiled his half smile with just the hint of white teeth. "You liked that?"

"I could feel the heat on my horse's belly."

"And did you like the way a bullet sounds? Did you like that?"

"They weren't shooting at you," said Jacob.

"I know." Ashby shook his head. "But they did their best to get you."

"You might have told me," said Jacob.

"You never know," said Ashby. "Sometimes you'd think I was just another rabbit to be shot and put in the poke. And the next time—the next time you'd think I was something to be saved forever."

"And the next time they do all their shooting at me." Jacob brushed his hand through his hair as if to brush out the bullets. "I might not have come."

"And miss the fire?"

"It was just like you were sailing through the air—and then just stayed up there."

But Ashby was ready to go on now. "Are you ready? Same as before. Just watch for my signal."

"I'm always ready," said Jacob.

The way led across an open field where the sage stood yellow-stemmed above the frost. Ashby led the way quietly across the field pale with frost and moonlight, still save for the sound of the horse. The breath steamed and was lost. Small gray birds scattered in front of them. A red fox came out of the darkness behind them, went past them without looking to the right or left, and disappeared into the darkness ahead. And beyond the field was a wood where the night had always been.

They got off the horses here to lead them through beneath the branches. Beyond the wood was an open field and then woods and then brush. Jacob could feel the night stretching out forever over this wood and over this field. This was how he would spend his nights. He would never sleep again. He would follow Ashby through the night—and over the fire. He would follow him to the Devil. And the air would hum with the wings of bullets.

Now the way led back to the silver river and the path ran alongside beneath the gray and white mottled sycamores. The river foamed and gurgled. Glistening frogs plopped—like that!—from the mossy bank into the water. The red glow ahead grew until it filled the sky.

And then they were there. Ashby raised his hand. Jacob stopped for what seemed a long time with eyes only on Ashby. Sometimes the breeze would bring wood smoke and laughing and low voices and the sound of voices along the river. Sometimes great sparks would sail into the air and glow like firebirds to drop tired and pale at their feet.

Ashby signaled Jacob forward. Now he could see. There was a picket line with bayoneted sentries and beyond was the great camp of tents and wagons and horses and artillery stretching as far as you could see. There was no night here.

Ashby pointed to a large tent with a cluster of flags in front. "Can you read that?"

It was a regimental flag of dark blue with a gold eagle and gold letters. It hung loose among the tassels. Then suddenly a breeze came and stretched it out—"2nd REGIMENT, STATE OF MAINE" it said in gold.

"Did you see that?" answered Jacob. "That's what that soldier was with, the one I told you about."

"Those are fine colors," said Ashby. "Fine colors. I would dearly like to have those colors."

Jacob shivered. He had gotten hot riding, and now they had stopped and the cold from the river was creeping into him. "General Jackson told me in particular for you not to be foolhardy."

"General Jackson should be a good judge of that," said Ashby drily.

"It's a handsome flag," said Jacob.

"And who's to expect us? We can be in and out before they know what's happened. They can't shoot for fear of hitting each other."

"They're not going to shoot at you anyway," muttered Jacob.

Ashby wasn't listening. "You see that bush there. It blocks their view. We'll go in along that line, and when I give the signal, come on fast. I'll take the standard. And if I miss it, you get it. We both can't miss. Then I'll make a sharp cut to the right, and we'll be off. . . . Are you ready?"

"I'm always ready," said Jacob.

CHAPTER X

THE STANDARD

It was at that instant as they started forward that they heard the horse coming up very fast behind them. Quickly Ashby turned his horse down the bank and into the river. Jacob followed, and when the horseman came, they were well hidden below the path in the dark shadows where the river eddied in white foam about the horses' legs.

Beat-, beat-, the horse went along the path until, "Halt! Who goes there?"

"Friend."

"Friend of who?"

"Friend of the Union."

"Pass, friend."

Ashby pulled himself into the sycamore and then climbed high into the tree. There was the sound of a bugle coming bright and gay from the camp.

"Listen!" Ashby said. "They're moving out."

"Yes," the bugle said. "We're moving out! We're moving out!"

"I bet that's Hannibal," said Jacob, and he swung himself into the tree. And it was Hannibal very clearly, standing in front of the tent, and already there were soldiers up, tents opened.

Jacob slid down the tree after Ashby. "Hannibal is really blowing them awake."

"I can hear him," said Ashby.

"I wonder where they're going."

"We'll find out."

"We'll follow them. That's what we'll do, isn't it?"

"Take too long," said Ashby. "We'll just ask them. If you want to know the answer to a question, you ask it."

"How will you ask it?"

"What's the password?"

"Friend of the Union."

"Aren't we just as good as any Yankee? We're going in the front door, and maybe we'll have a little breakfast." Ashby pulled a large dark poncho out of a saddle bag and put his hat in. The poncho covered all of him down to his boots. Jacob found one like it for himself. "Let me do the talking," said Ashby, "and I'll show you a Union camp." Ashby led the way up out of the river and along the path to where the campfires bloomed.

A blue-coated picket with a bayoneted rifle stepped onto the path in front of them. "Halt! Who goes there?"

"Friend," said Ashby.

"Friend of who?"

"Friend of the Union."

"Pass, friend."

The pickets didn't even look up from their fire as Ashby and Jacob passed by. They rode through the lines and into the camp where there was a rush of activity. Horses were being saddled. Wagons hitched up. Tents were coming down. Fires were being doused, and the steam came up and swirled about them.

Ashby stopped a sergeant who was leading a sleepy squad of men toward the headquarters tent. "Just came in from picket duty. We're looking for coffee."

The sergeant saluted. "I think you can get some behind the headquarters tent, sir."

Ashby returned the salute. "Thank you, sergeant." When they were out of earshot Ashby said, "I've always said that this Yankee army was a well-mannered army." Ashby rode along as unconcerned as if he were looking for a cup of coffee. They went by the headquarters tent and around to the side. Ashby gave a fond look at the blue and gold standard that fluttered there.

Just then Hannibal came out of the tent. He went by Ashby and he went by Jacob. And then he looked up. "Hey!" said Hannibal, "aren't you . . ."

Jacob didn't wait. He spurred his horse forward between the two tents, knocking over the tent struts as he went. The tent collapsed, and he could hear men struggling and cursing inside.

"Come back—stop that man . . ."

Jacob didn't know where he was going except that he knew he didn't want to stop. Ashby went by in a streak. He had the standard of the Second Maine like a lance in front of him. "Let's go, boy! We won't wait for the coffee!"

There were shots. "He's got the standard! Get them!"

They raced up one roadway and then down another. Men chased them and then dodged out of the way as Ashby and Jacob circled around and came down upon them. At one point they had to ride through a large tent where officers were struggling awake. One man had just got out of his cot when he saw Ashby in his black poncho on his white horse bearing down on him. The man fell back into bed and pulled the blankets over his head.

"This way!" called Ashby as they came out of the tent, and he took his horse like a bird over a gun carriage. Jacob followed. It seemed forever that he hung there over the gun carriage before he came safely down on the other side.

And they were out of the camp into the sudden darkness. There were shots. The darkness was eye-blinking. Only Ashby's white led the way. Ashby in his black poncho was lost to the darkness. They seemed to be on a road now. There were horses now behind. Jacob could hear them coming. And when it was a straight place he could see them bunched black across the road. They filled the road with horses' legs and hats and arms.

And now it seemed to Jacob that he was in a dream and no longer moving. Ashby seemed to be slowly pulling away in slow motion. And behind him they were slowly gaining. And he was not moving. Only the trees were moving fast. Now when he looked back there were white faces straining with their mouths open. Jacob had never seen faces like that. He had never seen anybody want anything that much. It wasn't just him they wanted, or even Ashby.

They just wanted. And they screamed for it.

They would run over him.

"Help me! Help me!" Jacob shouted into the wind. But the wind filled his mouth and took his breath away. And they came closer.

Jacob could not wait. He wanted off the road. He wanted out. He suddenly twisted his horse off the road. It was too sudden. The horse stumbled. Jacob fell. The horse disappeared down the road, with the bridle swinging free.

Jacob was in the ditch. What did he shout? What did he say? He was on his knees. His head was full of falling. He tasted mud. The poncho was a weight.

And then they were upon him, but they kept going. In the darkness they did not see him. Dimly they could see the horse ahead, and they kept going. As soon as they were out of sight, Jacob struggled up the bank that ran along the road there. The poncho came down to the ground. He slipped out of it. A ground-hog hole almost tripped him, and he stuffed the poncho down inside. What would that old ground hog think when he tried to come out that door?

He stood for a moment on top of the bank. He had not realized before that the moon had gone and there was no light in the sky except the white bellies of the low clouds. Sky and earth had almost closed up. There seemed very little room for Jacob. But he had to get away from the road. He took a sight on what seemed a low hill in the distance. There was thunder now. It shook the very ground.

A wind came up and drove the sky closer to the ground. It roared through—stopped—and left Jacob leaning foolishly against nothing. And then it blew again to take his breath away. When the rain came it came sideways and stung his face and went down his collar and flattened his pants against his legs. But it tasted good and washed away the panic of the road.

A streak of lightning lit the world. A clap of thunder shook it. For the first time he saw where he was, on a great wide plain without trees or brush and the hill he had headed toward was no hill but a black cloud bulging. The lightning ran along the ground like the trail of a big cat. And Jacob licked the rain. Let it lightning and thunder. He had not been frightened, he told himself. He had given them the slip.

And then it was that in the lightning he saw them and saw that they saw him. In that flash he saw one rider stop and point toward him. In the darkness after the flash he knew they were after him.

He ran. His wet pants flapped. His shoes made squidgee noises. Maybe he would run himself to death. And when the lightning came there was still no place to go. He could hear the horses coming now. The screaming white faces were crawling up his back. He kept running. He would not be down when they came.

The splashing hoofs came closer.

They were on him.

He felt an arm about him. He struck out.

"Easy, boy, easy." It was Ashby. He had come from nowhere and swept him up. The others were almost upon them. Jacob settled himself with his arms about Ashby from behind. He could feel the buttons through the poncho. With his cheek against the wet poncho he could feel the muscles in the back.

"Are they still close?" asked Ashby.

"They're still close," said Jacob. He didn't have to turn his head to know.

"And that's as close as they're going to get tonight," Ashby said.

Jacob felt Ashby's legs press the sides of the horse. They surged forward. There was no horse in the world that could catch them now. The white lengthened his stride. The horses behind were lost in darkness and then finally lost in sound.

"You all right?" asked Ashby. "I didn't know where you were."

"I'm all right. I fell. That was all." He shivered. He held his arms as tight as he could around Ashby to take the trembling out of them.

"We'll be there soon," said Ashby. "It's not far now."

"With the army?"

"No, not tonight. Tonight we'll spend by ourselves."

And it was soon. Ashby never lost his way once in the darkness. "There," he said, "is what you look for. That thorn tree that's blown over and grows along the ground now. In a short piece we'll come, we'll come to a place where some rails are stacked against the face of a limestone cliff. There! You see!"

Ashby dismounted, and they took the rails aside. The dampness of a mountain's insides came out from behind the rails. They led the horse into the darkness.

"In my saddlebag," said Ashby, "there's a flint and candle. Light it."

Jacob did. He held up the candle and the shadows danced in the biggest cave he had ever seen.

"Listen! *Ashby! Ashby! I am here!*" Ashby whispered the words soft and clear.

And the words came back. The cave said soft and clear, *"Ashby! Ashby! I am here!"*

CHAPTER XI

THE CAVE

AND IN THE CAVE were many things. There was a stall for the horse and hay. There were lanterns on the walls of the cave to be lit gold and fill the cave with dancing shadows. Ashby found the wood and brought it to the place where old ashes lay damp and gray. The fire caught, and the smoke was swept away toward the back of the cave.

"That's a real draft," said Jacob, pressing his hands toward the fire.

"This is a big cave," said Ashby, bringing more wood. "No one knows how big. That smoke goes out the other end of the cave. It could come out in West Virginia. It could come out in Ohio, that smoke."

"Ju-ju-just goes on and on, doesn't it?" said Jacob, shivering now that he had the front of his hands warm.

"Need some dry clothes for you," said Ashby. He rummaged around in an old trunk. "This is what I was looking for," and he held up a long jacket with matching pants. It was a handsome long gray dress coat. There were gold buttons and raised black embossed lines that ran around the buttons and from button to button and up to the shoulders where the gold braid was and up to the collar where the gold stars were.

Jacob had his clothes off and was standing wet and shivery. Ashby held out the coat for him. "Might be a little big," he said. It almost reached to the ground. "Just fold up the sleeves and it'll do."

"It's a fancy coat, all right," said Jacob.

"Do you know whose coat that is?" said Ashby, toasting himself against the fire. The steam rose from his pants and mixed with the smoke on its way to Ohio. There was the rich smell of drying wool. Ashby had his poncho off and his jacket opened. It was the first time that Jacob had a real look at him. Ashby was tall and wiry with slim grace. He was younger, too, than Jacob had thought. His grace was his authority. "That's Old Jack's coat! That belongs to the General himself!"

"It is an able coat," said Jacob, wishing he had a mirror. He tried to make do with his shadow on the wall.

"General Stuart gave it to him. The General wore it once, and it raised such a fuss that he gave it to me to keep for him. The only thing he said was, 'The General Stuart is very kind, but I'm afraid he is a little extravagant.' "

"The General wouldn't go for all that gold." Jacob shook his head. "Anyone would know that."

Ashby brought over a coffepot and a frying pan. "There's nothing like a little chase to make a man hungry." The coffee steamed and the bacon sizzled, and after the bacon there was salty ham and then potatoes cut up and fried brown, and coffee. And then put-up peaches in golden syrup.

"Given to me by a lady in Winchester," said Ashby. "We were on our way in a rush, you might say, and there was this lady with this jar of preserved peaches, standing in the street like this with the peaches held up like an offering for us as we went by. Never noticed the shooting. I went right by her. Then I looked back and there she was still standing there in the street, holding out that jar of peaches toward me with the Yankees bearing down. 'Yankees or no, I'm going to let that lady give me those peaches,' I said to myself. And I did. I just turned and went back, picked up the peaches with one hand, rode right on through the Yankee horse coming in the opposite direction, and went out of town at the other end."

Jacob took another helping of the peaches. "It was a good thing to do."

Ashby smoked his cheroot and looked into the fire. His eyes were sad again.

Jacob leaned back against a rock and patted his newly rounded stomach and wiggled his toes against the orange flame. "I think that was two dinners I ate tonight. I forgot I ate at home."

"Did you?"

"I don't think I ever did not spend the night at home," said Jacob. "I think this is the first night I ever spent away from home."

"You're homesick," said Ashby, stirring the fire so the sparks flew up. "It's what the new boys always are."

"No," said Jacob, "that's what made me say it. It's the first night I ever spent away and I don't miss anything. 'Course"—he leaned forward—"it's not as if I'm alone or as if there wasn't a lot going on this night."

Ashby stared into the fire.

"What are they going to think when I'm not there in the morning?"

"Your mother and father?"

"My mother and sister. What are they going to think?"

"That you're out coon hunting."

"They're going to worry."

"And probably right, too," said Ashby.

Jacob shook his head.

"You'll just have to do what you think right," said Ashby. "Not that I would advise you. I know what you're talking about, you understand, but it was a very long time ago for me. I guess if I tried real hard I could conjure up how it was with me when I first went in the service. But it wouldn't be of much account, because that's long past, but you know I wouldn't be surprised if . . ." Ashby went over to the trunk and came back with an old box. "Yes," he said, coming back to the fire, "here they are." He gave Jacob an old photograph. He looked at it carefully first. "Yes, I almost had forgotten. That's my father and my mother, Dorothea. It's a good likeness."

"Nice-looking people," said Jacob.

"And very good people, too, I think." Ashby looked into the fire as if he had lost something there. His black beard glistened and his dark eyes bored into the fire. Only his hands moved, one against the other.

Jacob, too, stared into the fire, but for him it was just a fire. Nothing danced in it for him. And then he saw another photograph where it had dropped by Ashby's side. Jacob could see it very clearly on the ground.

It was a young Confederate officer standing martially in a photographer's studio with a snow-topped mountain behind him and a waterfall. He was standing in the awkward stiff pose of all soldiers in all Civil War photographs, but for all that he was not stiff and awkward. His half smile said that. It said, "This is the way soldiers stand. This is how a hero looks." But his eyes said in a very serious way, "I am a soldier. I am a hero—never doubt it." Not boastfully, but the way you would say, "I am a farmer. I am a postman." Unchangeable. Unafraid. The snows would never melt on that mountain or the water cease to fall or those eyes change. They would look out like that forever.

Ashby saw the photograph for the first time and picked it up. "Yes," said Ashby, "that's my brother."

"I thought it was you," said Jacob, disappointed.

"And that's my brother's elk skin," said Ashby. He pointed to a great skin that covered the chair in the photograph and fell in folds to the floor. "Always had it with him. He killed that elk in the far west. Fighting Indians."

"And your brother," said Jacob. "Where's your brother now?"

Ashby put the picture away. "He was killed. Near Big Cacapon."

They stared into the fire when Ashby sat down again. Ashby stared into his side. Jacob stared into his side. Ashby lit another cheroot and blew smoke rings toward the fire. His jacket was open. On his suspenders ladies in pink tights rode plumed horses around a circus ring.

"Never have seen elk," said Jacob.

"It took five men to kill him," said Ashby. "And they ran when I came. He wasn't dead. They had run their horses over him. But he wasn't dead. He took a week to die. He had ten wounds in him, but he took a week to die."

"Your brother doesn't come back? He's not here?"

Ashby shook his head. "I used to look for him. But he's not here."

"I thought maybe everyone came back. Everyone that died."

"No, not everyone. I guess only the ones who liked soldiering."

"But he liked soldiering—you can see that. He was a real soldier."

Ashby nodded.

"But maybe—maybe he changed," said Jacob thoughtfully. "Maybe he got his full of soldiering."

"Don't see that," said Ashby.

"Maybe. I don't know." Jacob threw a piece of pine bark into the fire and watched it flame. "He doesn't come back. And if he's like he was in the photograph he would come back, wouldn't he?"

Ashby nodded again. "He was younger and had one more tie to break than I."

"Maybe," said Jacob, thoughtful again, "maybe he took too long to die. Maybe that was it."

Outside the wind came up and cried against the opening.

"Could be a lot of things," said Ashby as he got up and stretched his legs. He took a big thick gold watch out of his pocket. "It's almost four and time to get some sleep." He found a big blanket for Jacob. And then for himself he found a big heavy gray elk skin.

He rested his head on his saddle. Jacob could not take his eyes off the elk skin.

"It's the same one," said Ashby. "It's the same one as in the picture."

Jacob didn't say a word. It was the biggest elk skin he had ever seen. It was the only elk skin he had ever seen.

"Good night," said Ashby.

"Good night," said Jacob. And he watched the shadows on the wall turn into sleep.

It was the cocking of the gun that woke Jacob up. Ashby was up with revolver in hand going toward the entrance to the cave. Jacob followed. He never knew how Ashby had wakened or what he had heard, but there was Ashby at the opening of the cave peering out through the rails that hid the entrance. There was a Yankee soldier coming. He was coming up the hill toward the cave.

It was Hannibal.

And he stopped quite still in front of them. In the daylight Jacob recognized the path. It led out of the Big Sinks over the mountain to where he lived. It was the way he had shown to Hannibal. That was where Hannibal was going. He was going back to see if he could find Jacob and his standard. But now he was stopped here as if he were studying the pile of rails against the cave opening.

"That's Hannibal," whispered Jacob.

"He's after the standard," said Ashby. "That's what he wants."

Hannibal seemed just then to look right at them—and took a step toward them.

Ashby raised his revolver.

Jacob held his breath.

Hannibal looked, shook his head, and turned up the path toward the mountain.

CHAPTER XII

THE BATTLEFIELD

HANNIBAL STOPPED ONCE as he came over the hill and saw the battlefield. It was really as he remembered it—or as he expected to see it. The sadness was that quite clearly it did not remember him. He had remembered this place so well that it seemed to him it must belong to him, but as he came down the hill he knew only that he was returning to a dream.

The place was now a smooth gaunt meadow leading flatly from the road and then up the bare hills to where the trees stood in line along the top. Hannibal stood for a moment on the road looking up the hill to where the trees stood like a wall of gradual green on top. Crocus blossoms, dropped from the sky, lay forgotten on the road.

Hannibal climbed the fence and struck out across the moist ground—across the tufted old grass of winter, over the dark-green new short pointed grass of spring. The empty hay pens stood here always. He kicked the old piles of winter cow droppings and scattered them across the field. Behind he left circles of pale yellow for the sun.

This was where in that battle in another spring the bugles had blown and the drums had rolled and the companies had assembled in long waving blue lines. The first cannon shot had dropped aimlessly out of range. And you knew that now was the moment to move quickly and firmly forward—and, of course, you didn't. Everybody knew it—from Hannibal to the General. But you didn't. That wasn't the way it worked. Hannibal waited with the rest, until finally somehow the whole line went forward at once in a long slow walk. But already the oneness had been lost. They had come up the road in a column together, talking of coffee and the home of a pine forest for the night. Talking of those who kicked in their sleep and must sleep alone. Talking of those who built shelters that fell down.

But now in the changing from a column to a line and in the waiting, each had become alone. And each went up the hill alone.

Up, way up, in the line of trees there were scattered flashes of blue smoke and the sound and the shells exploded here and there in the wet ground far away and didn't count. The line went forward with you, and you kept up with the men you didn't know on either side. And then you started going faster. "Forward—hi!" the bugles blew. "To the top of the hill we go!"

And the whole line began to spread out until there were worlds between you and the next man. The line of trees had turned into a wall of smoke, and now the shells plowed the ground and flew the wet earth in clods of acid-smelling mist. Finally the whole line was running forward now. Some dropped when the clods hit them. Some dropped down to fire at the hill, firing and loading feverishly.

Hannibal had gone forward with the rest, running madly with his canteen flopping against his hip, and then dropping to the ground with the rest—to watch. To watch a few go forward and drop like old clothes. Was the bugle blowing now? There was nothing between the single dark blade of new grass at his nose and the hill so far away.

Hannibal held the rifle out along the ground in front of him waiting. There was nothing to fire at except a blue wall of smoke. And now there was the wet thud of rifle bullets. And even some like Hannibal waiting would suddenly turn from their stomachs to their backs and lie with knees up, looking foolishly at the sky.

And then there was no one alive ahead.

Hannibal had been running today.

Now he lay panting on the wet earth in the silence. The earth was warm with the sun. He fitted it. His heart thudded a pocket for itself in the wet earth. His fingers found hand holes.

Suddenly while he was still lying there, he saw

her come out of the smoke and the waiting trees and run with skirts held high in her hands down the hill. Hannibal stood up slowly and waited with his hands in his pockets for her to come down the hill. She was out of breath when she came, and the last of the way she walked and fixed her hair with both hands raised to her head. As she came closer, she came more slowly with the words on the tip of her tongue waiting until it was almost a whisper the way she said them. "I thought you were hurt," she said reproachfully. She stuck her hands firmly in the front pockets of her longish dress and made it billow out.

"I fell," Hannibal said. "I was just going up the hill." He wondered why a blue-and-white gingham dress made her cheeks so pink and why her throat and neck were made of warm marble.

"I was on the hill looking for ginseng," Gray said.

"That's where I was going."

"But," she said, almost at the same time, "you're a soldier, aren't you? I mean, you are a soldier. And I didn't know why you were there."

"I just came by."

"There haven't been any soldiers here since the battle."

"Wouldn't think so," said Hannibal.

"And not all alone, either."

Hannibal didn't answer but simply started up the hill. He was suddenly very tired, and he just wanted to get to the top of the hill. He wanted to get to the top of this hill so that he could look down. He walked doggedly ahead. He stumbled once.

"You are hurt," she said.

"I'm not." He walked ahead very quickly now, leaning into the side of the hill.

Gray had to run with quick little steps to keep up. And then she would ask, "Why did you come here?" He would go ahead without answering. Then she would run, catch up again, "What do you want here?" she would say.

He was already at the top, looking down, when she came up the last steep part over the ridge of earth that ran along the top of the hill. He just stood there, looking down.

Gray slipped coming up the bank and fell down. He kept looking down the hill. She did not have the real feeling that he had come for her. "You could help me, soldier," she said.

"I'm sorry." Hannibal reached out a hand and pulled her up. Gray felt that she might fly.

"Well," she said, turning so that she could look down the hill and see it just as he saw it, "I don't know why you wanted to come up here so much just to see that."

Hannibal turned to her. He was a little bit taller than she. His eyes were that pale brave blue. "Seems that strange to you?"

"Well, yes, it does." She was a little taken aback. The blue eyes made the question seem abrupt. "Yes, it does. Here you come along the road, and then out onto the field and fix your gun, and then come running along as if it was a charge."

"Well, I suppose," said Hannibal.

"Suppose what?"

"I don't know," said Hannibal. "Except you ask a lot of questions."

"You don't answer many of them, do you?" Gray wondered why he had not come on a horse if he was going to carry her off. She was not sure that he was going to. She wasn't even sure that she wanted him to—except that he had come.

"No, ma'am," said Hannibal. "We don't ask so many questions where I come from."

"What would happen if I asked you where you come from?"

"I'd answer you quick and fair."

Gray waited. "Well?"

"Well, ma'am?"

"Where do you come from?" Gray spelled it out slowly.

"Maine. I come from Maine." His blue eyes looked at her in question.

"I've seen it on the map."

"And my name is Hannibal, Hannibal Cutler." He almost smiled. "You didn't even ask me that."

Gray stuck her hands way down in her pockets. "And you never asked me my name, either."

For an answer Hannibal sat down on the breastwork, stretching his feet in front of him. He pulled out a piece of hardtack, and without saying a word or even looking at her, he reached it out to her.

"Well, I never!" Gray said. She wondered if he was shy.

"Why don't you sit down?" he said, without turning around. "I was going to ask your name and I would have. It's just that I'm not good at people telling me what to do and particularly not females."

"I guess you don't have many females in the Army." She said it sadly for his being so deprived.

"I guess we don't," he said enthusiastically.

"My name's Gray," she said. "Gray Downs."

"There goes one," said Hannibal. "See him go."

"That's just an old ground hog." They watched the ground hog hump across the pasture, come to his hole, stop, stand up and look around, and disappear.

Hannibal sighed. "I'd like to shoot some ground hogs. It's been a long time since I shot a ground hog."

"And I suppose you came all the way up this hill just to shoot some ground hogs?"

"No ma'am. I didn't say that." He reached out a hand. "Maybe, ma'am you better give me back that piece of hardtack. You might just break a tooth on it. Or find a worm."

Gray knelt down beside him, a little bit in front of him. "Where are you going, Hannibal Cutler?" she asked. "Where are you going?"

CHAPTER XIII

GROUND HOGS

GRAY ALMOST used up one of those two kisses then. She would have if Hannibal had not said, "There goes another one."

That made her sit down with her chin on her knees. If she had been alone she might have cried. Instead she bit her knee through the gingham. They sat there like that without anybody saying anything for the longest time. Hannibal wondered how the best way would be to find out if Jacob had come home with the standard. Gray certainly wasn't going to say anything. She didn't even know why she stayed.

"You are the quietest person I ever saw," she said.

"I expect," said Hannibal.

Gray patted the ridge where they sat. "This is where the South was, and down there were the Yankees. It was one of the big battles of the war."

"Not much of a battle at all," said Hannibal. "It was a very little battle."

"And I bet you haven't seen the cemetery down the road. Rows of crosses. South on one side of the road and North on the other."

"In a big battle they just dig a big ditch and toss in the bodies all mixed up."

"Everybody around here says it was a big battle." Gray had only brought up the battle because she thought it would interest him and it hadn't worked at all.

"It wasn't."

"You'd think you were here, you know so much about it."

Hannibal got up and stretched. "I'd like to have been here with them coming up the hill. That would have been shooting."

"I think it's terrible," Gray said. "All that shooting and killing. We still find bones sometimes making garden. And bullets. There are bullets all over."

"Is that right?"

Gray took him over to where an old chestnut stump stood rotting. "See the holes there."

Hannibal scooped up a handful of the rich brown tree dust from the bowl of the stump. Sifting it through his fingers, he came upon a gray, flattened bullet. "That's one all right. Right spang in the tree and been here all the time." He bit into it. Then he flew it far down the hill.

His cap fell off. Gray picked it up. She looked at it closely. "Second Maine. Why they were in this battle here! I've heard that."

"I expect they were," said Hannibal, reaching for his cap.

"That's why you came," said Gray, stepping back out of his reach, putting the cap on. "You wanted to see where your people fought. I knew it was something about the battle. That's what it was, wasn't it? You wanted to see where your people fought."

"Of course it was. I could have told you that." He said it a little impatiently, for he could see the blue-coated troops moving in a line up the hill and how easy it was to shoot them from here. There was no place for them to hide. They were baggy blue, and their faces didn't matter. One minute they were running and the next they were still. You picked one out. The sights picked one out. It didn't make any difference which one. They were all the same. One or the other. North or South. It was only afterward, walking among them that they were different at all.

The victory was in the shooting of them, not walking among them when they were dead. The pity was that they would not, they could not say, "You killed me. I'm dead. You're alive." They could not even say that.

Hannibal reached for his cap. This time she did not move. She had stood absolutely still as he stared down the hill. She stood now as he took the cap roughly from her head. "It's so still suddenly," Hannibal said. "Do you see how still it is and the field so empty?"

The field was as it had always been where the empty hay pens stood like ships. Gray put her hand in her hair where his hand had been and did not put it back in place. "They told you—your father, your grandfather—they told you about the battle and that's how you knew, isn't it?" With the tips of her hair she could feel where his hand had been.

"There goes another one," said Hannibal. He lay down on the parapet with the rifle out in front of him. "It's easy shooting from here." The stock was warm against his cheek. It was hard against his cheek. He caught one in his sights and followed it slowly. Fired! "Got him!" Hannibal said.

"I don't know why you want to shoot ground hogs," Gray said. "They never did anything to you."

"They make holes in the meadows," Hannibal said, reloading. "Your father, your brother, ought to shoot them."

"That's not why you shoot them."

"Why do you shoot anything?" Hannibal said, getting into position again. "Why do you shoot anything?"

Gray knelt down beside him. "Please, don't."

"Watch that one. When he gets to his hole he'll stop and stand up just for a minute—watch! See him! Got him!"

The round little ball of fluff popped into the air as he was hit. He rolled a little bit down the hill and lay still. "That was shooting," Hannibal said and rolled over on his back to stare at the sky.

"I hope you're finished," Gray said.

"I'm finished."

They stayed like that. Hannibal stared at the sky. Gray smoothed out wrinkles from her skirt.

"Do you believe stories—like someone coming down the road—or things happening to yourself? Things that haven't happened before to you—but are going to? Do you believe stories like that?"

Hannibal squinted at the sky. "I believe stories about myself."

Gray bent over to get between Hannibal and the sky. "And do you think that someone might just come down that road—and carry me off?" She had said it. She sat back.

Hannibal closed his eyes. "Could."

"Someone handsome. Someone rich. Maybe someone just passing through going West. Maybe his people own California. Maybe he can't get back to California until he's found me. Maybe he just has to wander and wander until he finds me."

"That's a lot of maybe's," said Hannibal.

"But could be," said Gray leaning over him again. "It could be true." She tried to see behind his eyelids. "It could be someone might come along."

She kissed him lightly. Hannibal opened one eye

and closed it. Gray sat up straight and hugged herself. She smoothed out wrinkles. She had never kissed before. She had never known what lips were for before. She would kiss rocks. She would kiss the bark of trees. She would kiss her toes. She could see far away.

She could see across the coves to other hills, where the new grass crowned the tops dark green, and beyond to the mountain that lay on this side of the Big Sinks. Gray had seen this many times. The dark green on the hills and the new pale leaves and the hill sides speckled with dogwood and service trees. But never before with someone on the hill had she seen it or felt the sun on her head and on his eyelids at the same time.

The sun went through her to her heart and opened it like a blossom.

"Are you real, Hannibal?" she said. "Are you real?"

"Real?" He sat up.

Gray thought he was going to kiss her.

But he only held her hand so hard she cried. "I'm real," he said.

She rubbed her hand. It hurt.

"I didn't mean to hurt your hand." He reached out now and put his hand on hers as if she might be made of china.

"I'm real," she said.

Hannibal was sitting up looking down the hill

again. He rubbed his eyes against the sunlight. "I was looking for your brother," he said.

"So you know I have a brother?"

"I know. And his name is Jacob."

"Now you tell me where you saw him," said Gray, kneeling close by him. "You tell me, because his mother's half worried to death he's run away."

"She better."

"He has run away then, hasn't he? I knew he had. He was in his bed and then in the morning he was gone, and he's not a boy who gets up when he has just anywheres to go."

"He's got something of mine," said Hannibal, "and I want it back."

"Is he in trouble?"

"He's in pretty mixed company."

"Jacob, Jacob," Gray said. "Why do you do this?"

"He'll probably be all right," said Hannibal hastily.

Gray wiped her face with her skirt. "I wasn't going to cry."

"I didn't say you were, but you were sure clouding over."

"What will I tell my mother?"

"About his running away?"

"About going off to get him. What will I tell her about where I'm going?"

"You can't get him." Hannibal shook his head. "There isn't any way you can get him."

"He's off with the soldiers, isn't he?" said Gray. "That's where he is. He's off with the soldiers."

"Never said that." Hannibal got up and stretched. He buttoned his jacket.

Gray looked down at the grass. And in a whisper she said, "He's off with Ashby, isn't he?"

"I don't know anything about Ashby."

"I do. He rode a white horse, and he was on that hill there they say like a statue in the battle. Jacob's told me. Sometimes he's said he's seen him and sometimes he's said he heard him. And I saw the Spring Rider yesterday and I saw you today. And Jacob saw a soldier yesterday."

"I'll try and get Jacob back for you," Hannibal said. He reached out and pulled her up.

"And you're one of them, too," she said. "You've come back to fight like the others. I wanted you to be real," she said and hammered at his chest. "And you're not, you're not!"

Hannibal put his arms around her tight so that she couldn't hammer at him. "Don't ever say that. Don't ever tell me that."

CHAPTER XIV

MR. LINCOLN

HANNIBAL LAY with his head in Gray's lap. She traced the curve of an eyebrow. Her fingers memorized his chin. She tucked his hair behind his ears.

"I think," said Gray, "I am going to cut your hair."

"No girl," said Hannibal, "is going to cut my hair."

"That's silly. Who's going to do it?"

"We have people. Some of them are pretty good, too. The only thing I'm afraid of is you never cut hair. I might lose a pretty good ear."

"I cut hair," said Gray firmly. "How do you think I have my scissors and comb in my pocket? I was going over to neighbors to cut hair today. I'm maybe one of the best hair cutters around. And I've never seen a head I'd like to get my scissors into like yours. You sit here on top of this log and be still. You've got knots like a dog with burrs."

"I think you want to cut my hair so you can put a piece in a locket and say, This is Hannibal."

"Yes—I can say, This burr belonged to Hannibal." She pulled.

"That hurt!"

"Of course it did."

"Or you can say, Here's an ear, one of Hannibal's two ears. He had only two, and I've got one."

"Will you hold still. Do you want your hair cut or no?"

"How do I know you ever cut hair? Have you got any samples of hair you ever cut? Little pieces that belonged to somebody—little pieces of somebody you carry around with you?"

"Faith, Hannibal Cutler. Now really sit still."

"Why don't you use the scissors instead of pulling it out?"

"When was the last time you had your hair cut?"

Hannibal didn't answer. He closed his eyes. He could feel the sun on his cheek. He could feel the scissors like snippy wings. He wished he could stay like this. He caught some of his hair in his finger tips. Snake skins.

Gray laughed. "They won't know you when you go back."

"I'll tell them I had a fight with a bear."

"No, you look fine. You look much better." Gray brushed off his shoulders. "I wish I had a mirror."

"It's better this way," said Hannibal. He reached for his cap. "At least I have this."

Gray put her scissors and comb back in her pocket. She stood for a moment behind him with her hands on his shoulders. She was going to say, "Maybe you won't have to go back," when she saw the figure on the road. "Look!" said Gray. "Down on the road. It's the Spring Rider."

"I see him."

"I knew he'd come again. He'll know how to get Jacob back." She took him by the hand. "Come."

Hannibal shook his head. "You go. I'll stay here. We're not meant to see him. Not meant to talk to him."

"How can that be? He was the President. That's silly."

"Court-martialing isn't silly."

"How can you be court-martialed just for talking to him?"

"Well, you can. I guarantee." Hannibal left no doubt.

"Just because he wants to stop the fighting?"

"I guess. Even if he is the President. But you go. You should go."

Hannibal watched Gray run down the hill. She held her skirt high and her hair tossed, and that was how she ran down the hill to the rail fence along the road where the Spring Rider sat waiting. And he tipped his hat when she came and held out his hand.

Gray talked and he nodded. She pointed up the hill and he nodded. She put her hands over her face and she wiped her eyes and he nodded. She pointed out the hill where Ashby had been seen like a statue on his white horse. Then the Spring Rider got his long legs over the fence, and he and Gray started up the hill toward Hannibal. Hannibal thought he would not wait. Why had Gray done it when he had told her? But he did not leave his place by the old stump. He wanted to get a good look at the Spring Rider. He had always wanted to see him.

He was a real tall man. He cast a long shadow. He carried that stovepipe hat in one hand. He walked slowly with his head down, the better to hear Gray, who never stopped talking. He took long slow steps as if he was thinking, and his long black coat was wide at his knees. Sometimes he looked up and searched the edge of the woods where Hannibal was. His face was long and sad and ugly. His clothes were black and baggy. His shirt was a white triangle at his throat. A gold watch chain looped like a bright snake in and out of his vest.

When he got a little closer, Hannibal backed into the woods.

"Hannibal! Hannibal! Where are you? I know he's here," he heard her say. "I know he is. I know he wouldn't go no matter how mad he is for my bringing you up here."

Hannibal went farther into the forest. He could

see them now at the top of the hill. The Spring Rider sat down on the stump. Hannibal could see Gray running back and forth. "He's just hiding. I know he is. He wouldn't have gone without saying he was going."

The Spring Rider stood up. "Maybe I should go. I was afraid he might not linger." He had a high voice.

"He really wanted to see you."

"It could be he's afraid to see me."

"No, he isn't, I know."

"I'm going to go," said the Spring Rider. "It's a lot more important for you to see him than me."

"Oh, Hannibal," Gray said, "please—"

She wasn't going to get him to come out that way, Hannibal thought as he came out from behind his tree and through the trees with his head down.

"You see!" Gray said. "You see!" And she held out her arms to the Spring Rider to show she had made a tree into a man and brought him out of the woods. She took Hannibal by the hand and she took him to the Spring Rider, and she put him up so close that she could step back and leave them safely together. The Spring Rider held out his big hand. Hannibal shook it firm, and it shook back firm but without showing off. It was a very big hand.

"Sergeant."

"Sir," said Hannibal.

"You see," said Gray.

The Spring Rider sat back down on the stump. "I understand you're pretty familiar with this ground."

"Yessir, I am." Hannibal looked down again over the field.

"You have the advantage of me, sergeant. I saw all my battles coming off a telegraph key." He looked at Hannibal. "That's a fine bugle."

"It's issue," said Hannibal. "Just issue."

"Never had anything like that in the Army I was in."

"Were you in the Army?" said Gray. "I never knew you were in the Army."

"Not in the sergeant's Army. Long before that, in what is called the Black Hawk War."

"Is that right?" said Hannibal.

"Fighting Indians, no doubt," said Gray.

"Fighting mosquitoes was more like it," said the Spring Rider. He settled down on the stump and stretched his long legs out in front of him. "I'm afraid it wasn't much of an army. But I served for eighty days and I earned my hundred and twenty-five dollars."

"But," said Gray, upset a little with his lack of seriousness, "you are—I mean—I know you are Mr. Lincoln."

"I am."

"Then I don't know what right they had to make you fight Indians and mosquitoes for eighty days and a hundred and twenty-five dollars."

"Oh, they didn't make me. I was a volunteer. A captain of the volunteers. I don't believe the mosquitoes ever had such a target. I remember one night when I was trying to sleep and these two beasts landed on my thumb and they started eating their way up my hand and up my arm. 'Hairy devil, isn't he?' one of them said. They ate their way up my arm going slower all the time until one said to the other, 'Enough is enough,' and he dropped off. The other said, 'It's California or bust.' He dropped off at the elbow."

"Mr. Lincoln says that he and you will get Jacob back."

"I said we might venture it if you were willing." Mr. Lincoln looked up at Hannibal.

"You won't be much welcome out in the Big Sinks—by either side."

"That sounds familiar."

"I'm coming, too," said Gray.

Hannibal looked at Mr. Lincoln. Mr. Lincoln studied a stick he was whittling. Hannibal shook his head. "There's no place for girls out there. No place at all."

"Well, suppose . . ." said Gray.

"And no supposes."

"It might be—" said Mr. Lincoln, getting up and brushing the shavings from his lap, "it might be you could come a way with us—just a way, you understand."

Gray looked up at him, as if to wonder how far she could press it, but Mr. Lincoln only shook his head. "I'll just be a minute," she said. "I'll have to tell a story to my mother and then I'll be back. You'll wait?" And then she was gone running through the wood where the sun lay in patches. Running fast, she passed from room of shadows to room of light—and was lost over the hill.

Hannibal shook his head. "Mishandled, if you'll excuse it."

Mr. Lincoln looked still in the woods where she had been. "Compromise, sergeant. Remember that. When you can, and especially with the female, compromise." He settled down again on the stump. He looked closely at Hannibal. "You're not eighteen, are you?"

"I'm one of the over-eighteens." Hannibal smiled for the first time.

"Over-eighteens?"

Hannibal sat down and took off a shoe. Then he took a tiny piece of paper and wrote something on it. He put the paper inside his shoe. He put the shoe back on. Then he stood up. "I'm sixteen, you understand, but when they ask me, I say 'I'm over eighteen,' and then they let me in." He took off the shoe and took out the piece of paper he had put inside. He handed it to Mr. Lincoln. "Eighteen, you see. All I said was—'I'm over eighteen.' Did you ever see anything like that ever?"

Mr. Lincoln shook his head. "Never. It must be what they call having a foot for numbers."

Hannibal laughed. "I'm going to remember that. That is good. Foot for numbers!"

"I doubt if that trick would have worked in Illinois."

"Work anywheres," said Hannibal. "Iowa. Pennsylvania. Vermont. Knew heaps of Vermont boys who did it. Work anywheres."

Mr. Lincoln pulled his big gold watch out of his pocket.

"She is taking her time," said Hannibal.

"Oh, no," said Mr. Lincoln. "It was just habit. Like everybody else I look at the watch. Not that I'm going to do anything about it. I just look at it. She's a fine girl, though. Deserves a good man."

"She's going to take him to California," Hannibal said.

"Did she say that? That shows you how honest she is. Most of them wouldn't tell you where you were going until you crossed the state line."

"It's not something I need very much," said Hannibal, "California." Absentmindedly he took the bugle to his lips and blew a half note.

"Blow it, Hannibal," said Mr. Lincoln. "Blow it like you do when you call them to the Big Sinks."

"This is the bugle that does it. This is the one."

"Come to me! Come to me!" it cried and it reached down the valley and down the road.

Mr. Lincoln shook his head. "That would bring the dead, wouldn't it? I can see them coming to that."

"It brings 'em," said Hannibal.

"And does it send them? That's what I want to know—can it send them away? Can you say, 'Good night'?"

"I could," said Hannibal. "I could blow them all away, and me included, forever."

"You could."

"I could."

"I thought you could," said Mr. Lincoln. "I just wanted to be sure."

"But I'm not about to, you understand," said Hannibal.

"Look," said Mr. Lincoln. "There she is." And there she was—in a bright gay dress with white bows and she looked different all over.

Hannibal was going to say, "About time!" but then he looked again. And instead he said, "Why, you look fit for inspection!"

CHAPTER XV

ALONE

JACOB WAS AWAKE. Jacob was asleep. Jacob was dreaming. Jacob was climbing in the old dead pine tree. Gray was there with Ashby. And Jacob was climbing to be with them. It was day. It was night. The trunk of the tree was wider than his reach. The trunk of the tree was thin as a pole. The two of them had gone on without him. And then Jacob slipped. He reached out. There was nothing to hold on to. He was falling. The slipping tree was going up and up, faster and faster. There was Ashby's beard. Jacob reached. For a moment he held on—and then the beard began to pull away from the face, began to pull the face away from the head. It came off. Jacob was falling. Jacob was falling, falling.

Jacob was awake. He was in the cave. He remembered now. After Hannibal had gone by they had had breakfast, and then Ashby had said that he had to go and report to Jackson but that Jacob was to stay there. Jacob had wanted to go too, but Ashby had said that they only had one horse and he would go alone, but that he would be back. "I'll be back," he said, "and it will be worth waiting for," he said, "and I want you in the cave," he said, "all the time."

Jacob had done that. He didn't know how long he had done that. He had eaten some more. He had walked a little way exploring to the back of the cave. He had not gone outside. He had looked through the rails piled against the opening, but he couldn't see very much and he hadn't seen anybody. After he had done all that, he had gone to sleep. That was when Ashby's beard had come off and that was when he woke up.

And that was where he was, awake in the cave. He went to the opening. It was late in the day now. The sun was balanced on a line of black clouds to the west. There was no one in sight that Jacob could see. He did go out. It was bright. And the air was sweet. Where was Ashby? There was not a very good view of the Big Sinks here. The cave was too low and all that could be seen was a few sink holes rising to a small ridge.

Jacob didn't dare to get too far away from the mouth of the cave in case Ashby should come. He had spent all day doing what he was told, and there was no point in spoiling it now. He would stay in the cave. He would be in the cave when Ashby came. He would be able to say that he had been in the cave all the time, which was true because the only time he had not been in it was now when he was planning to go back in which was the same thing as not being out at all. Jacob took one last look at the sky and went back in.

He remembered as he stepped back into the cave the way Ashby had called when they had arrived. Now Jacob called, "Jacob! Jacob! I am here!"

And the words came back. The cave said loud and clear, "Jacob! Jacob! I am here!"

"Colonel Jacob Downs!" tried Jacob.

"Colonel Jacob Downs!" said the cave.

"General Jacob Downs!"

"General Jacob Downs!" said the cave.

Jacob was suddenly speechless. Gray. And his mother. What would they think when he did not come back? When Ashby returned, he would have to tell him that he had to get a message home. He probably should go back right now, but he couldn't until Ashby returned. And Ashby would. There was no question of that. So he would stay in the cave until then. But that was all Ashby had said. He didn't say anything about what part of the cave, did he? And it was a big cave, wasn't it? And when Ashby came, he would be able to hear him. And what else was there to do anyway?

Jacob put on his old clothes. He didn't think it right to go off in the cave in the General's uniform. Besides it had occurred to him that maybe Ashby had gone off to bring General Jackson to give him a medal and maybe General Jackson wouldn't like the idea of Jacob in his coat. Jacob wondered how a medal would look on his own jacket.

Jacob took a lantern and walked toward the back of the room which got narrower the farther he went. The green moss was deeper. It got darker. It got wetter. And then finally the way narrowed down to only a slit. Looking back, Jacob could still see the opening of the cave. And he went on. He squeezed through an opening. And then he was into a much smaller room, a lower room.

The moisture dripped from the ceiling. Bats hung from the ceiling. Gray bones of something lay rotting on the floor. No one maybe ever had been here before. Jacob could feel the mountain arched above. Maybe there were people up there on the mountain now who didn't know that Jacob was down here underneath them. Wouldn't they be surprised if they knew, if I, Jacob, went up to them and said, You're up here and do you know where I am? I'm way, way down below, underneath you!

Jacob noticed that the room seemed to slant up. Maybe it came out on the top of the mountain. It came out someplace, or there wouldn't be such a draft. He still hadn't gone very far. It wasn't as if he couldn't go back any time he wanted to. It wasn't as if he were lost. So he went to the end of that room.

And then there was another passage, much smaller, through which he had to crawl. And he crawled through that.

He had to crawl slowly to keep the lantern ahead of him. But even so he was surprised when he put his hand ahead of him that it suddenly went down into a mud, into a slime. The lantern slipped. It fell into the same slime and went out. He had no way to relight it.

There was no question of going forward now. All he had to do was to back up, get into the room he had just come out of, then find the passage back to the main room. That was all. He did back his way out of where he was.

There was nothing to see. His eyes turned into fingertips, and he felt his way along the wall. It was smooth in places, and mossy, and wet, and the bats squeaked on the ceiling. The worst was the stumbling. He shuffled. And he bumped his head.

And then he found the passage. He could reach through with his arm. That was it. He worked his way down that. It seemed much longer going back than it had before, but of course he had had the light before. He stopped, hoping he might hear some sound from the main room. He went on. His feet were wet now. His clothes were wet. He was hurrying. He wanted to get through. His hands came up against a wall. There was only an opening now around his knees.

He was lost. He had taken another passage somehow. But there was a good breeze coming through the small tunnel ahead of him. He began to crawl through that. Something crawled across his hand. He strained to see. With his tongue he licked around his mouth to see that it was there. He shuffled forward on his knees. The passageway got smaller and smaller until he was stretched out inching his way through a tube. The whole mountain pressed down upon him. And when he breathed, his breath came back in his face. His shoulders were ten feet wide. Now he wasn't going anywheres or coming from any place. He was twisting inside a tube.

And then suddenly ahead—Was it a light? It seemed a light. And he remembered the way to tell would be to open his eyes and look. He had forgotten whether his eyes were open or shut. He would open his eyes and look. It was there. Something was there. He closed his eyes. It wasn't there.

He pushed and twisted himself through the tube. The light was there. And it wasn't very far away now. He was out of the tunnel. He could crawl now easily. The light was ahead and bigger. It came in gashes through the mountain. Jacob had found the other end of the cave. Wait till Ashby heard about that! Wait till—!

He had slipped. Almost at the entrance he had slipped. One leg was caught in a crack. He pulled. It was stuck. He couldn't reach it with his hand. A fallen rock was jammed against his ankle. He had fallen forward and the rock was behind him. He pulled until he could hold his breath no longer, but it was no good. He was part of the mountain now.

He was stuck. The light came on a shaft of fresh air.

He was stuck. He could reach the light almost with one hand.

"Ashby! Ashby!" he called. "It's Jacob! Jacob! Jacob! I want you, Ashby."

There was not even an echo.

CHAPTER XVI

KING OF THE LICK

THE WAY took them along a white road sunk between high gray split-rail fences on either side. The late afternoon sun threw the zigzag pattern of fence upon the road. The summer ahead lay in the first hot dust of the road, and the spring was in the moist banks. In the distance was the mountain rising like a long wall between them and the Big Sinks. The white service trees and the dogwood dotted the mountain. Toward the top the trees still stood bare in grayness, and the granite backbones stood out sharply.

The Spring Rider rode ahead. Hannibal and Gray walked behind. Sometimes there were long silences filled only with the sight of white clouds sailing across the big sky or a lamb with its head poked between the rails looking down at them.

And once there was a rush of wind and twenty or thirty lambs—only lambs—bore down on them from a hill. The leaders stopped abruptly, and those that followed piled in upon them in a tumble of white fur and pink noses and black hooves. There was butting and shoving until the leaders took charge—jumping straight up on stiff legs, jumping over other lambs—and led them back the way they had come. Again they came back, blocked now by a stump, and again they came, stopped now by a butterfly, and turned again in a rush of stretched legs up the hill. And then they did not come back again.

Hannibal and Gray talked. Like lambs butting, they talked. Coming together, backing off, shaking themselves. Hannibal talked of things he liked to eat and not and people he had known. He had heard Daniel Webster once on July Fourth, and he puffed out his chest like a rooster and threw back his head and roared. Mr. Lincoln said it was a remarkable demonstration. Hannibal told of a time when he had been lost on a beach at night, caught between the rising white roaring waves and a dark bank too steep to climb. The seaweed clung to his legs. White sea gulls swept calling out of the darkness.

"You must have been scared to death," said Gray.

"I was," said Hannibal and found another daffodil for her collection.

Sometimes they talked at once. "Did you think that?" "That's what I thought, too." "Same exact thing happened to me."

Hannibal had never really thought that there was anybody very much like him, not that he was better, or worse, but just that there wasn't anybody who had lived like him and certainly not anybody who wanted to hear what he had to say. Not that he had ever tried it before. And certainly not with a girl. The thing that was good about girls was they came from their place and you came from yours. You would expect a girl to be scared to death lost on a beach at night. You would expect a girl to carry white daffodils flopping on the end of long green stems.

The sun stopped in the sky. The zigzag fence shadows were painted forever on the road. The white clouds hung becalmed in the big sky. The forsythia was no longer new in yellow. The forsythia was yellow forever. Spring had not come. Spring was.

They stopped once in the shadow of an old barn.

You would expect a girl to bring you mint cool as silver from the brook to be bitten from her hand.

"They make very able rails in this country," said Mr. Lincoln.

"You split rails," said Gray. "Where did you split rails?"

"That was in New Salem, Illinois. I guess I could split rails with any man. That was what my friends told me, and I believed them, even when it got me into trouble."

"And how'd it do that?"

"There was a gang there called the Clary's Grove gang, and their champion was Jack Armstrong. My friends, wishing to see me get ahead in the world, let on that Jack Armstrong was nothing to me. Now Jack was short, I probably could have licked salt off the top of his head, but he was wide and he was able."

"And you licked him," said Hannibal.

"I did," said Mr. Lincoln. "And the others came after me. I just stood back—'I'm the King of the Lick,' I said. 'You come on.' "

"I'm surprised," said Gray.

"It's what they wanted to hear," said Mr. Lincoln.

"That's not why you said it."

"You're right, it isn't. But I meant to ask the sergeant why he enlisted, when he was only 'over-eighteen.' "

"I don't know," said Hannibal. "People all about were pretty up about the war and all. I've thought about it. I think it was that we didn't want them to leave us. We didn't want to take them over. We just didn't want them to leave us. That was it."

"That sounds reasonable," said Mr. Lincoln. "It's in accordance with my own feelings. And now even though it's over, you don't want to stop."

"That's something else," said Hannibal. "That's not what we were talking about."

"No, I didn't think it was," said Mr. Lincoln. "What you're talking about is that I'm-King-of-the-Lick feeling."

"Maybe," said Hannibal.

"That's what Jacob thinks he is. He thinks he's King of the Lick," said Gray. "Always has."

"Maybe always will, now," said Hannibal.

"You mean because he's with Ashby?"

Hannibal nodded. "I don't expect you leave Ashby once you've ridden with him."

"Jacob wouldn't go without saying good-by—I know he wouldn't."

They didn't say anything else after that. The afternoon was over. They followed the road into the mountain, and from the sudden shadows came a cool breeze from beneath a million trees. Looking back they could see the wide valley waiting for the night. The mist was gathering in the lowest hollows.

The way led up the quiet mountain in the growing darkness. And when they reached the top the whippoorwills were with them, and it was dark.

And suddenly there below them in the blackness of the Big Sinks was a great golden circle of campfires.

"Yes," said Hannibal. "See the fires, Mr. Lincoln. That's the Army of the Potomac. I thought they might not have moved too far."

"How do you know it is?" Gray said. "Maybe it's General Jackson."

"I know," said Hannibal, his eyes riveted to the circle of campfires below them. He wanted to be part of it. "I'm going down there," he said.

"But you can't," Gray said. "You can't. We have to find Jacob."

"I'll come back." Hannibal was getting his gear together.

"You won't. You know you won't. You'll get back with them and you'll forget."

"I said I'd come back."

"You won't come back," Gray said. "You'll be just like the rest of them."

"I am," said Hannibal, suddenly very serious again. "I am like the rest of them. I told you that."

"But you're not. I know you're not," Gray said fiercely. "Don't let him go, please," she said to the Spring Rider. "Tell him!"

Mr. Lincoln shook his head. "Tell him? You don't change the wind by holding the weather vane. Let the sergeant find for himself how the wind blows."

"Well," said Hannibal.

"I was thinking," said Mr. Lincoln, "as I watched the sergeant look at those campfires, of my friend Offuts' hogs."

"Hogs?" said Gray.

"Yes," Mr. Lincoln said. "Mr. Offuts had some hogs and we were going to take them by river barge to market, but they wouldn't go on. We drove them and we drove them but they wouldn't go across the planks onto the barge. And then someone said if only they couldn't see the water we'd be all right. And we sewed up the eyes of all those hogs, and then we drove them slick as can be on to the barge. And I was thinking that the only way you could keep the sergeant away from that circle of campfires is to sew up his eyes like Mr. Offuts' hogs."

Gray said nothing. She fiercely wiped away the tears. She was out of tears.

"Let me go with you," Gray said. "I'll go with you. I'll help you find Jacob."

Hannibal shook his head. "You don't believe me? You don't think I'll come back?"

"I do—yes, I do, but maybe, maybe something will happen—and you can't—Oh, I don't know. Maybe you won't be able to." Gray looked suddenly around. "Mr. Lincoln! Where did he go?"

"I don't know," said Hannibal, turning around. "He was here."

"Just like that—he disappeared. That's what you'll do. You'll disappear. That's why I want to go with you."

"You can't disappear like that," said Hannibal.

"Please, let me come with you."

Suddenly Hannibal took her hand very hard.

"You are real—aren't you?" said Gray. "You're as real as me, aren't you?" And with her hand she took in the two great circles of firelight breathing in the Big Sinks below. "That frightens me, but you don't. You're different, aren't you?"

Hannibal looked out over the Big Sinks. "I don't know," he said. "Maybe I am. Maybe I just think I am."

"I would come," said Gray. "And I will come, if you don't come back."

"No," said Hannibal. "I'll come." And he kissed the top of her head.

"That's two kisses," she said.

He turned once to look. He saw her raise her hand that held the long-stemmed daffodils. He thought he saw them dip white in the night, and then the trees were in between.

CHAPTER XVII

THE PASSWORD

HANNIBAL WENT down the lowering path. He was not sure what he was going to do after he found the Second Maine. But he would be able to borrow a horse, if it was only from the artillery. And then there was the hope that someone might have seen Ashby or Jacob. He would find out where they were, and he would get a horse. And he would go back to Gray and—well, anyway, it would work out. Once he got back to the Second Maine it would work out.

Hannibal stopped. He thought he heard a sound. He thought it must be the Spring Rider, but it wasn't. It wasn't anything. Where had Mr. Lincoln gone? He wasn't the sort of person to disappear like that. Hannibal quickened his step. It was worrisome. Mr. Lincoln was all right, but everyone knew he was out to stop the fighting. And Mr. Lincoln knew, too, that Hannibal had the power to do it. Hannibal could blow the tune that would end it forever.

That was true. That was how it was. Hannibal

called them—and after their time each spring they went their way. But if Hannibal were to do it—were to blow the tune—he would blow them all away. That would be the end, for all springs. Hannibal had never played the tune. He had never been told what tune it was, but he knew it was there. Then there would be no more armies, no more war, no more Ashbys, no more Spring Rider—and no more Hannibal. Hannibal frowned.

Hannibal smiled. Hannibal smelled coffee. He smelled bacon. He smelled biscuits. He smelled horses. He heard harness. He heard wood being split. He heard heavy feet. He smelled tobacco. He heard voices and laughing.

"Halt! Who goes there?"

Instinctively Hannibal dropped to the ground. He had not seen the sentry who was outlined so clearly now against the firelight.

"Who goes there?"

"Friend," said Hannibal.

"Friend of who?"

Hannibal had forgotten. It seemed as if it had been days since he had been with the Army, when it was only that morning he had left. He could hear the hammer being cocked, but he knew that it was too dark for the sentry to see him clearly.

"Who goes there?"

"Friend."

"Give the password. Friend of who?"

Was it Friend of the Union? Was it Friend of Gray?

"You're no friend of mine without the password. Identify yourself!"

"Sergeant Hannibal Cutler—Second Maine."

"Who is your commanding officer?"

Commanding officer? "How do I know?" shouted Hannibal. "I can't remember now." He couldn't remember anything. "What difference does it make?"

"I don't know you, soldier! I never heard of you. Come forward and surrender!" Hannibal could hear them whispering now. "He's sure not one of us. Let's get a squad together and bring him in."

Hannibal backed away until there was a patch of brush between him and the camp. They wouldn't come after him. It wasn't worth it to them. He would have to try and find the Second Maine. He would be able to get in there.

Hannibal circled around and came back to the camp in another place. He could see the regimental standard here of the Fourth Wisconsin where the officers were sitting before the headquarters tent smoking their pipes and cigars. He could see them very clearly.

"Who goes there?"

Hannibal didn't even bother to answer but slipped back into the night. The next time he came up against the pickets of the Seventieth New York.

"Who goes there?"

Hannibal could see the groups of soldiers by the fire, playing cards. The Army was not concerned about attack tonight. The fires blazed and most of the men were lying around the fires. There were only a few pickets out. Hannibal could hear the low roll of the voices of the men by the fires. He had never been beyond the pickets looking in before. He had never been on the outside before. The voices had the casual drone of men who had said this all many times before. It was punctuated occasionally by short explosions of laughter and then resumed its drone.

He would only have to find the Second Maine and he would be all right. They wouldn't care about the password when they knew who it was, when they knew it was old Hannibal Cutler. But he couldn't find the division. He saw all the others. He saw the famous Sixth Michigan and the Tenth Ohio. He saw Colonel Dunbar of the Twenty-third Vermont, standing in front of his tent, looking up at the sky. Dunbar had lost an arm at Fredericksburg and his life outside of Richmond. Hannibal had heard Dunbar say once that sometimes he was driven mad by an itching place on his missing hand. It was worse than a place you couldn't reach on your back. You couldn't reach this at all.

Hannibal circled around. Hannibal had never known the Army was so big before. It was a city. A city on the move.

"Who goes there?" That was a Maine voice for sure.

Hannibal stepped out of the shadows into the edge of the glow. He could see the pickets. He could see the command tent where the gold and blue standard had stood.

"Stop! Who goes there?"

"Friend."

"Friend of who?"

"Friend of the Second Maine."

"Identify yourself."

"Sergeant Hannibal Cutler, Third Squad, Fifth Platoon, Company B, Forty-fourth Battalion, Thirty-third Regiment, Second Maine." He remembered everything now.

"So you're the Hannibal Cutler we've heard about."

"You've been looking for me, have you," said Hannibal happily as he came forward. "You missed me. You missed old Hannibal Cutler."

"We missed you all right, and you stay right there."

"Why should I stay here? You think I have bugs or something?"

"I don't know what you have, soldier. I'm just doing what I was told."

Hannibal didn't like standing there like a prisoner or a criminal. "What's the idea?" he said. "I want to come in." And then across the camp between the fires he saw the military police. They were coming toward him. He shouted, "I want to come in!"

He backed away.

"Hold it!" said the picket.

"No-o-o," said Hannibal, as he backed into the darkness step by step.

The picket was waiting for him but not to shoot him. Hannibal was at the edge of the light when the military police came. Then he jumped—into the darkness.

"I'm not coming in. You understand that? I'm not coming in at all!" said Hannibal's voice.

"Just stay where you are and you won't get hurt!"

"No, I'm not coming in. Line up! Line up! I'm not lining up any more or eyes left or eyes right any more. Just me! Hannibal Cutler! I don't know what's wrong with you but I don't care. You made your mistake. And it's just me, now. Just me."

And then he began to run. He could hear them saddling horses and commands shouted. He had to find his place. He found a path up a rock ledge. They would never look there. The horses would not be able to get there. He followed the path as far as it would go. He could hear them coming out of camp. They were below him. He could hardly see them. They seemed to pass, and then he heard one soldier—it sounded like one soldier—come along after the rest. He heard him pause. He heard him start up the path.

Hannibal waited. He could see the soldier now. In blue. In baggy pants coming crouching along the path. Hannibal slid his gun forward so that it was in front of him. It had not occurred to him before that he might shoot. He had not thought of that. But they were not going to capture him. They were not going to do that.

The soldier had stopped now in the path. He looked around. He was familiar. But Hannibal could not see his face. The soldier had his gun ready. There were just the two of them. And then suddenly the soldier jumped to one side. He had seen Hannibal. And now there was nothing for Hannibal to see but just the tip of a gun barrel.

Hannibal waited. Then the gun he was watching moved. Hannibal waited for where the face had to appear. When that came he would shoot. That was what he waited for.

It came. A white face. At the very moment he saw himself beneath the cap he fired, because he had started to. He was shooting at himself. Fear is your own face.

How much can happen in a minute, in a second? He remembered smashed things. He remembered breaking windows and crushing eggs in his hand. He remembered saying to someone, "I hate you! I hate you!" He remembered a cat tied by its tail to a tree branch. He remembered throwing a rock at a big man's head. He remembered hiding on a wooded hill while they looked for him and called. He remembered killing snakes with a hoe. He remembered fish flopping for life in the air.

The face that was his came clearer. Frightened.

Hannibal shot and the world blew up.

And then he ran. There was no telling how far he ran. He knew the shot would bring them. He went up the mountain. Out of the Big Sinks. Away from all the armies. But he could not run forever. They had horses.

And then he saw an old chestnut above the road. It was a huge old rotting thing. He realized as he touched it that it was like a sponge. At the end where it had fallen, some animal had burrowed out a small home. It was here that Hannibal crawled, forcing his way up into the black tunnel, clawing out the inside with his hands, tearing out great hunks of the rotting sponge. Farther and farther he crawled into the blackness with his eyes shut.

He heard the horsemen when they rode by. Nor did he stop fighting his way up the tunnel when they passed. He pulled out the chunks of sponge and pushed them down with his knees. He went as far as he could go. He stopped and slept. There was no room for anyone else in this place. He had crawled to the end of the world. He slept and dreamed of climbing mountains.

It was the very middle of the night when Hannibal woke up. He shook his head to empty out the dreams. There was no sound. The moonlight lay in white triangles beneath the trees. His heart was pounding as if he had come running from a long dream. But he knew now that he had wakened and was in the woods on the edge of a small farm where the apple trees were out.

He remembered the face.

He was afraid.

He was afraid to lie still with his eyes open. He was afraid of the moonlight on the ground. He was afraid to close his eyes and go back to where he had been running. He was afraid that if he lay still he would not be able to keep up with his pounding heart. He had never been afraid like this before—in a very quiet wood in the middle of the night alone with himself. Dull gray fungus grew in the darkness on fallen trees. Even his toes seemed far away.

A whippoorwill cried from very close. What did the whippoorwill say?

A whippoorwill cried from very close again. What did the whippoorwill say?

Beyond the wood the fields were and the fields had fences around them. That was what he would do. He would build rail fences of split locust and chestnut. He would split the rails and drive the stakes and put up the panels ten feet tall. At the end of the day, before the sun went down, he would have closed a field with a fence of new rails eleven feet long with the panels ten feet tall. Then if you woke in the middle of the night you would walk to the edge of the field where the fence would be. No matter how dark it was or moonlight or how still it was, you could touch it.

And in his field at night would be whippoorwills with him. If it was too quiet he would walk where he knew they were in the heavy grass in the fence corners. They would cry after him as he went by. Round and round the field along the inside of his high fence he would go.

This is my night dream, said Hannibal to Hannibal.

It was then that Hannibal saw him—sitting on the fence below the wood, in full light, was the Spring Rider. He was casually slouched long-legged, and yet Hannibal knew that he had been waiting there for him all night.

CHAPTER XVIII

THE WHIPPOORWILL

"IT WAS YOU," said Hannibal. "You were the one." The fire bush was in the shadows, waiting for the sun which was inching its way by fingertips. The heavy blossoms hung down ready for the match.

Mr. Lincoln nodded.

"What did you do?"

"I found your Second Maine. They keep a very orderly camp. I let myself be seen. That wasn't hard. My headpiece is as strange as I am. And I enquired about young Sergeant Hannibal Cutler and where he was and how I had an appointment with him. That was all I did."

"That was enough," said Hannibal. "You knew where I was. You knew when I came back they'd be after me. You set them against me. You had no cause, Mr. Lincoln."

"I want the fighting stopped, Hannibal Cutler."

"And you set my friends against me. That wasn't

fair. I wouldn't have thought it of you. I wouldn't."

"That's because you don't know me. If you understood that above everything I want the fighting stopped, that I want the Generals and the Ashbys stilled—if you understood that, then you'd know I'd do everything and anything."

"I wouldn't have thought they'd believe you."

"You didn't think they'd chase you like an animal, did you?"

"But it's not going to make me blow them all away." Hannibal shook his head. "It's not going to make me do that."

"Maybe. Maybe not. But now you're alone. You're all alone. And you haven't been that before. You can't go to them. And you can't go back to Gray. You're not different. You told her you were different, but you're not."

"Maybe I am," said Hannibal. "Maybe I just am."

Mr. Lincoln got up and stretched. He took his tall hat off, and he put his tall hat on. "If you call the tail of a dog a leg, then how many legs would that dog have?"

"There's nothing to that," said Hannibal. "That dog would have five legs."

"No!" Mr. Lincoln clapped his hands together and the clap woke the night. "No! Just calling a tail a leg don't make it one. It's still a tail." Mr. Lincoln came over very close to where Hannibal was sitting on the fence and he bent down so that he blacked out the moon. "You have to know what you are, Hannibal."

"I said I'd go back. She expects me back."

"And what will you do then? Will you stay? Can you stay? How long can you stay?"

"We'll see," said Hannibal, moving away from the fence.

"You're dead, Hannibal Cutler, you can't stay. You can come back next year—for your few days—but you can't fight. You're on the outside now."

"She can come with me," said Hannibal fiercely. "She can do that. And you can't stop her."

"And Jacob can stay with Ashby. Yes, she can do that. And I can't stop her. But you can. Is that what you want? Do you want them to die never having lived so they can spend a few days with you each year? Is that what you want? What do you want, Hannibal Cutler? Don't you know yourself?"

"You're an old man," said Hannibal. "It's different for you. You don't care."

"That's not the difference. I'm an old man who knows he's dead. You're a young man who doesn't know he's dead. You think you're still 'under-eighteen' with roads and roads ahead of you. Blow the taps, Hannibal, say good-by. You're going to do it someday. You're not Ashby, or Jackson. You know something now they don't know. You can't pretend any more."

"Look! Look!" Hannibal said. "Down there, in

the old orchard. There's a boy down there. He's waving at us, I think."

But the Spring Rider was gone.

Who was the boy in the orchard? It was not Jacob. And yet he was familiar. He was a boy Hannibal knew. Knew from long ago. Hannibal didn't wait. He took off down through the woods after the boy. Hannibal climbed the fence. The night was cool. The moon was bright. In the white orchard he would find himself.

But the boy was not in the orchard. Hannibal searched the shadows. He waited quietly for a long time, hoping that the boy would show himself. Then Hannibal climbed the huge old apple tree that stood to one side of the orchard. It had been there before the orchard, and it looked down upon the neat rows of young trees. It was like climbing into the inside of a big flower. All the moonlight had been caught in there and given scent. It was like drowning. The blossoms were so heavy there was nothing to be seen. He hung on for dear life. The higher he went, the brighter the tree became. He was climbing to the moon.

It was from the very top that Hannibal first saw out. The boy was standing in the middle of the big meadow, looking back to the orchard. In the brightness of the moon the boy stood out dark in the rolling meadow. Hannibal remembered himself as a boy on a sand dune in the night like that. He had always remembered that—not from in the middle looking out but as if he were looking down from above and saw himself caught like a butterfly. He had seen himself that night.

Suddenly, the boy turned. Hannibal watched him cross the meadow, and then go along the run, and finally cross it with a great wide-legged broad jump. He landed on his knees. It was the second time Hannibal had ever seen himself. And then the boy turned up the road that ran over the mountain to the Big Sinks.

Hannibal followed. Everything seemed so simple now. He had forgotten the panic of waking up. He had forgotten the sound of Mr. Lincoln's high voice. He was alive. The Spring Rider was dead. All he had to do now was to cross the meadow, and over this fence, and to the willow following. The run was full. Pearls formed in strings around the rocks in the middle of the run. At night it made more noise. At night it was deeper. At night it was colder.

Hannibal scooped out the water first in his hand and then he lay full down beside the brook and drank. He drank great gulps. He lay with his head half in the stream so that the water ran into his mouth and out of it. The moon shivered on the run. He smelled new mint, and with his fingers searched for it, and finally kneeling, crawling along the bank following his nose, he found it and bit off leaves. He tore it up and stuffed his pockets. He was alive.

Now he had come to the place where the boy had leaped the run. It was the narrowest place along there, but still it wasn't narrow. It wasn't the water that bothered Hannibal. It was the falling into the moon that bothered him. He took two practice runs, and then he leaped—high he soared over the shivering moon into the moist grass on the other side. And his knee prints were farther than the boy's. "I guess that was a jump," said Hannibal to Hannibal.

The road to the Big Sinks ran along the run, and then together they disappeared into the woods. Here it was dark. The branches arched overhead. The only light was the light left from years ago in the sand of the road. Then above the noise of the run he heard something coming sharp-hoofed and stone-scattering down the road. Hannibal slid to one side behind a sycamore at the edge of the run.

Two small deer came down the road daintily and rubbed the air with their noses high. They stepped with high steps into the run and sipped. Hannibal could feel the water going down their long fuzzy throats in long silver streams. He wondered if they came every night like that. If they came whether he was there or not. He didn't want them coming if he was dead. If he was dead he didn't want them to drink.

He wondered suddenly why he didn't wish to shoot them. He didn't know why. He felt incomplete. It wasn't their fault, they were very pretty, but he threw a rock at them to send them scattering into the darkness.

A whippoorwill cried. "You're all dead," the whippoorwill said.

The road became steeper. It curved back and forth as it sought its way up the mountain. There were places now where the moon shone through. At one sharp open curve a single dogwood stood absolutely still, arching its branches up as if it were catching its blossoms fluttered from the moon and were afraid of losing one. From here Hannibal saw down the mountain over the treetops to the valley where he had been. He could see the brook twisting silver. He could see across the valley to the other mountain sleeping. He could look above him into the woods. There were no shadows for him now. He had become a night animal at home. He smelled pine. He smelled leaves left over from the winter. He was not tired. He was not an old man. He had found a night that had no end and was not dark for him.

Higher and steeper the road went. Into pines now and past a spring that ran out of the side of the mountain on a wooden trough. And past a gate that had no fence on either side. And past a gray stone chimney standing free and clear with a black mouth. And past a round sharpening stone on its stand with the handle raised, waiting for a hand. Beyond that in an old apple orchard gray boxes sat where bees had been. Just at the end of this place a flowering quince burst into fire. That was where the road began to go down. That was the top of the mountain where this farm had been and the fire bush planted long ago.

And that was when Hannibal saw him. Far below on the edge of the Big Sinks was a night rider on a white horse. Behind him he drew a saddled horse with no rider. And every once in a while he would stop and shout at the mountain.

Hannibal clambered down the road as fast as he could. Because of the way the mountain curved, he was able to get well ahead of the rider so that he was waiting for him.

It was Ashby. On his white. Ashby was in splendid gray with black slouch hat and high black boots. And in his lap was another gray uniform and a gray hat like the one he wore. And across the front of his saddle was a sword like the one he wore by his side.

Ashby stopped almost opposite Hannibal. "Jacob! Jacob Downs!" he called. "Where are you? It's Ashby! I'm here!"

Hannibal brought his gun to his cheek. And in his sights was Ashby. He ran the sights up and down the gold buttons, and with his gun he could feel the roughness of the buttons.

CHAPTER XIX
THE BUGLE

"JAA-COB! JAA-COB! It's Ashby! Ashby has a horse for Jacob! Ashby has a sword for Jacob!"

But the mountain didn't answer.

And Hannibal let the gold buttons turn away. He let Ashby's shoulders slump and turn away. He let him ride away. He watched him go. The riderless horse followed obediently behind. Ashby went out of sight. But Hannibal heard him again calling to the mountain, calling to Jacob with promises of horse and sword and the uniform he carried on his lap.

"Huh," said Hannibal to Hannibal. He hadn't shot the deer, and he hadn't shot Ashby. He had heard about Ashby. He had heard about him from men who had had Ashby in their sights and hadn't shot him, had let him go, like a many-pointed deer maybe, or like anything that there weren't two of.

It was then, or maybe a few steps later, that he heard a muffled voice. It came and went. It was close.

It was far away. It was in the air. It was in the ground.

"Ashby! Ashby!" It cried. "Please!" It begged. And then it was lost. Ashby had not heard it. He was out of sight.

Hannibal stopped his heart and listened. It came again. "Ashby! Ashby!" It called from the middle of the mountain.

Hannibal followed it. Up this way. No, over here. There, beyond that tree, behind those rocks, here—yes, here, from behind these rocks, the cool inside of the mountain came out here. He pushed the rocks aside. There was a hole. He put his head into the cool darkness. "Who's there?"

"It's me, Jacob." The voice was tired and worn but it was clear to hear. "I knew you'd come, Colonel. I knew you would."

"It isn't Ashby. It's Hannibal. Are you all right?"

"I guess, but I'm stuck. My leg is stuck."

"I'll get you out." Hannibal found a candle in his pocket. "The hole is big enough, I think."

"Where is Ashby? I thought I heard him calling. Didn't I hear him calling?"

Hannibal squeezed his way down into the hole that went sideways into the mountain. He lit the candle and shielded it against the draft coming from the mountain.

"I see your hand, I think."

"I'm here, over here. I can see you good."

"Where are you stuck?"

"It's my foot. I can't reach the rock that's got it caught."

"This one?"

"Yes, that one. You pull and I'll move my foot."

"Like that?"

"Yes . . . yes, that's it, now." Jacob sighed.

"Are you all right?"

"I'm all right."

"Let's get out of here."

They crawled out of the cave.

"I'm thirsty," Jacob said. He took a long slow drink from Hannibal's canteen. "That's good."

"How's your foot? It was caught pretty tight."

"It's all right. It's a little sore." He tried to stand and sat down suddenly.

"Let me see it," said Hannibal.

"It's not broken. I have to get back to Ashby."

"It's not broken much anyway," said Hannibal. "But I've got to get you home."

"I guess so," said Jacob. "I guess that's right. But listen! Do you hear that?"

The wind shifted.

"No, I don't hear anything," said Hannibal. "Come on, we've got to go."

"It sounded like someone calling me—from a long way off. It sounded like Ashby. I thought I heard it from inside the cave."

"You could hear anything being stuck inside a

cave like that. And how'd you get there anyway?"

Jacob told him as they went back across the mountain together. Hannibal had to half carry him with one arm around his shoulder. They often had to stop. Jacob talked and talked. He talked about how water tasted and how trees looked and how big the sky was and how he was probably going to live forever now and go round and round the world.

"I think if something like this happens and you don't die, then it means you're going to live for—for—I don't know how long. Don't you imagine?"

"Could be," said Hannibal. "Come on, we've got to go."

"I'm going back to that old cave someday and open it up," said Jacob. "It's probably stuffed with gold. And what I'll do with all that gold!"

"No idea."

"I'll probably become the richest man in the county. Richest man in two counties." Jacob looked at Hannibal carefully. "You think maybe Ashby's waiting at the cave for me? You think if I went back he'd be there waiting?"

Hannibal shook his head.

"I'd buy things for Gray, too," said Jacob. " 'You want it, Gray; you got it,' I'd say. Dresses and shoes and scents, too."

"How's the foot?" said Hannibal.

"I'm going back tomorrow to see if Ashby's there." Jacob looked up at the blue sky. "I think of those bats down there squeaking on the ceiling. They just don't know anything about what they're missing. Not me. I'm going to live to one hundred and forty-two. I'm going to have a hundred cows, four horses, six hogs, and ten children. A couple children."

"You're a planner," said Hannibal.

"Listen," said Jacob. He had stopped by the old white sycamore whose muscled roots split the run. "Did you hear that calling? Someone calling? Someone calling me?"

"It's the run," said Hannibal. "Noisy. Water's high."

Jacob followed Hannibal.

The sun was almost up when they came down the mountain to the log barn where Hannibal had come awake that other morning.

"I better stay here," said Jacob. "Gray will be down soon with the milk for the lambs. I want to see her first."

"You'll be all right?" said Hannibal.

"I'll be all right. But where are you going?"

"I'm just going," said Hannibal.

"You going back to the Army?"

"Suppose."

"What I don't see is why Ashby didn't come back. Why do you think?"

"Maybe something happened to him."

"He said he would, and I think he meant it. Don't you think he meant it?"

Hannibal had one of the lambs in his lap. It sucked greedily at his thumb. He ran his hand over the tight white curls. When he put it down, its legs were already running and it ran around the side of the barn and then back again.

"You going to see the ocean?" said Hannibal.

"See the ocean?"

"You said you were going to go around the world. You'll have to see the ocean."

"Well, I guess so then," said Jacob. "I guess I will then."

"That's good," said Hannibal. He got up and got his gear together. "You say good-by to Gray for me."

"I will," said Jacob, getting up and leaning against the barn. "But I didn't thank you for pulling me out of that old cave. I am obliged to you."

Hannibal left Jacob there in the new warm sun against the log barn. Hannibal followed the run to where the road started up the mountain. From there he could see the meadow that Gray would come through where the battle had been and the hay pens always stood like anchored ships.

And then he saw her standing in the grove of locusts beyond the meadow. He knew it was Gray. He knew from the way she stood, from the way the dress hung, from the way she straightened her hair. Her dress blew in the wind as if the wind were in love with her and could not stay away, as if the wind wanted to take her away with it wherever it lived. She stood there very straight, leaning against the wind a little bit. She stood with her back to Hannibal, and he wondered if she was smiling at the foolishness of the wind that thought it could do that and at the willfulness of the wind that it wanted to do that.

She came down through the locusts and into the new sun, and she left dark tracks in the dew where she had stepped out the diamonds. When she saw Jacob standing against the barn, she began to run, swinging her shoulders the way girls do when they run.

And Hannibal saw that from his place on the mountain.

He spit a couple of times. He wiped his lips—and then he blew. "Good-by, good-by, good night, good night," he cried. The call echoed up and down the valley. He cried "good night" to the new sun and diamonded meadows and girls with swinging shoulders and men on white horses and everything.

On the other side of the mountain the regimental colors fluttered patchily from toothpicks. And then they were gone.

ABOUT THE AUTHOR

In the mountains of Virginia, where John Lawson has spent many summers, the past and its legends are always close to everyday life. From this background, and from the author's reading in the diaries and memoirs of Civil War soldiers, came the tale of the Spring Rider.

A native of New York City, John Lawson was graduated from Exeter and Harvard College. During World War II, he served with the Army in France and Germany. Mr. Lawson was in the banking business in New York City for many years, and is now retired.

Mr. Lawson is also the author of YOU BETTER COME HOME WITH ME, a 1966 School Library Journal Best Book, about which *The New York Times* said, "Reading this book is like falling in love."